I0710617

# AXIOM

## A CARDINAL-WOOD STORY

## A. R. MILTON

ISBN (Print Edition): 979-8-99013-190-3
ISBN (eBook Edition): 979-8-99013-191-0

To my father and mother who raised me with love.

To my sister who is my friend.

And Karen for her unwavering support.

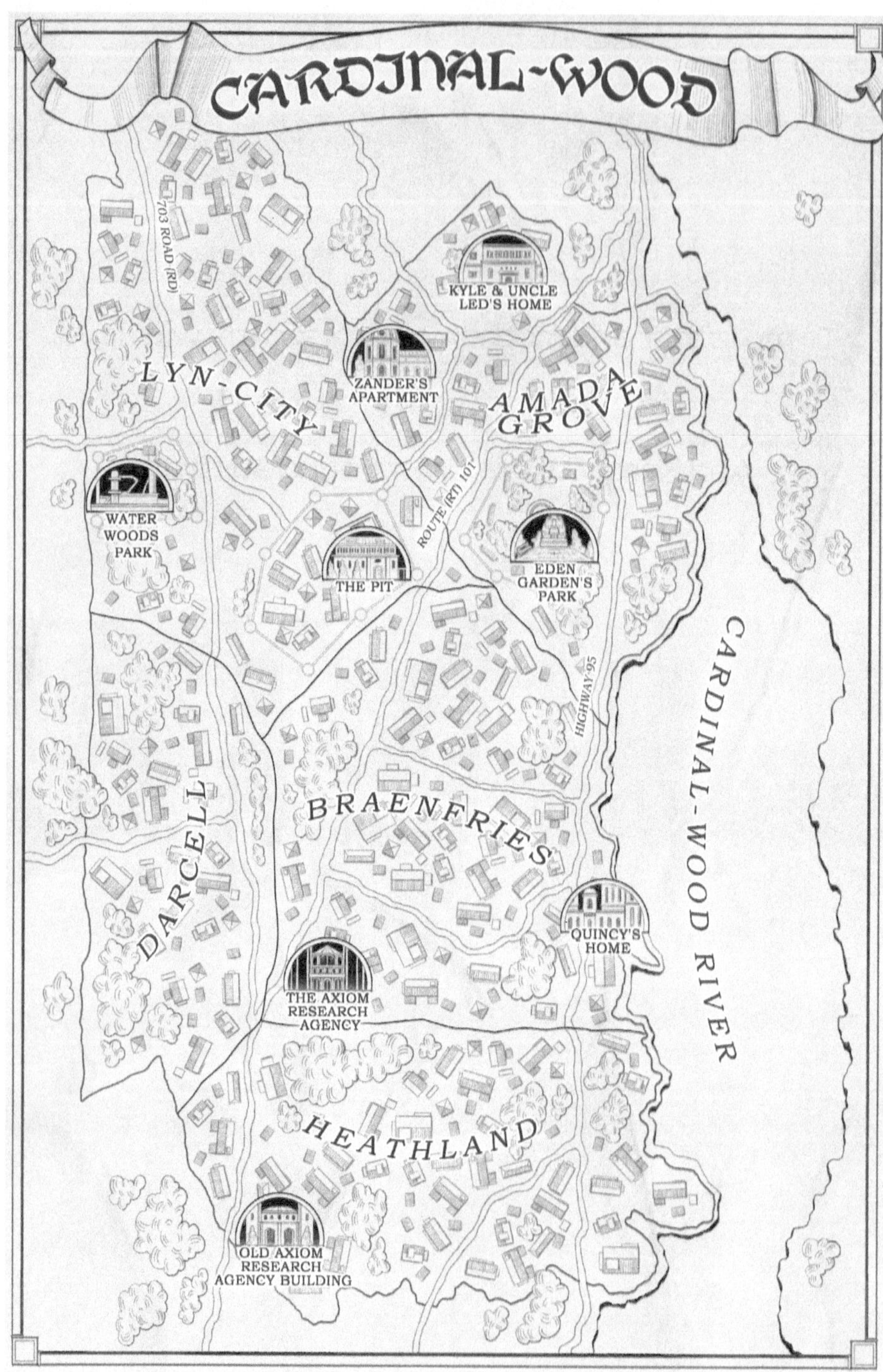

CARDINAL-WOOD
703 ROAD (RD)
LYN-CITY
KYLE & UNCLE LED'S HOME
ZANDER'S APARTMENT
AMADA GROVE
WATER WOODS PARK
ROUTE (RT) 101
THE PIT
EDEN GARDEN'S PARK
HIGHWAY-95
CARDINAL-WOOD RIVER
DARCELL
BRAENFRIES
QUINCY'S HOME
THE AXIOM RESEARCH AGENCY
HEATHLAND
OLD AXIOM RESEARCH AGENCY BUILDING

# 1

## ENTER THE PIT!

Eat. Drink. Sing. Leave your worries at the door and fall into … The Pit!

Zander Thurman slowly analyzed the chalkboard sign, giving his vision time to distinguish the yellow-and-pink lettering used to relay information at his place of employment. Below the welcome was a list of specials The Pit was offering for the day: $2 Corona, $3 Irish coffee, $4 rum smoothies. Zander shook his head in disgust as the numbers and letters of the drinks' names and prices blended together like some alcoholic's online gamer tag: *$2Corona$3Irishcoffe$4rum*. He ignored the food specials and continued through the front door.

The lighting in The Pit was, as its name suggested, dim with tinted windows that kept out any hope of daylight, even on a bright day like today. Zander's eyes adjusted as he crossed the threshold. The blood-red carpet was the first thing the blur in his eye could focus on. A man no taller than six feet and mildly husky stood behind the podium in the waiting area with his head down, scribbling with crayons on a napkin. Zander's eyes struggled to make out the host's name on the tag that clung to his red vest.

"Who changed the sign out there?" Zander asked as he walked toward the podium.

"The sign's been changed?" The man asked himself, more so than Zander. He scratched his head, hoping a memory about the change would surface.

"The Long Island Party bowl special is missing."

Kyle. Zander was close enough to see his name tag now.

"You're probably one of the few people in the city who enjoyed that, Zan. Besides, Bianca said she was takin' it down after a customer got into an accident last week," Kyle said, extending a fist. Zander reciprocated the extended fist to complete the timeless fist bump.

"That won't stop me from making my own," Zander said, smiling. "Is Bianca in today?"

"Yeah, check the kitchen. I think I heard her hollering at the cooks."

Kyle lightly tugged on the golden rope to his right that controlled the red velvet curtain behind him, partly exposing the dining area. Zander peeked through and spotted a couple in the far corner. They were early enough to the Sunday brunch special to be the only ones seated. Both happily shared one menu while an extra one lay lonely on the table.

Plates shattering behind the door leading to the kitchen on the right resembled a mini-thunderstorm loud enough to shake Zander back into focus.

"If you see a random girl walk in here dressed in a uniform send her to the back. It's my cousin's first day," Zander said, glancing back at Kyle.

"Say no more." Kyle tugged the rope, opening the curtain fully. "The Pit awaits you, good sir," he said in his best nasal butler impersonation.

The dining area of The Pit had the scent of wood polish and whiskey engrained into its wood floors. A red carpet leading from the entrance to the dining area overlapped the wood floor down the center, distinctly separating the room. Tables lined up on both sides facing the mini-stage the red carpet led to. As Zander made his way to the kitchen the sweet fragrance of lavender and honey—foreign to this place now, just as it was then—crept up his nostrils and took his mind to the night he met—.

"Zander! Shit!"

Bianca.

"You were almost late," she said wiping a stain off of her vest with a paper towel. The door that led to the kitchen was still swinging, creaking in pain from the force of Bianca's push.

"I don't have to clock in for another fifteen minutes. When we actually open."

She took her eyes off the stain and looked at him with a blank stare for two seconds before frantically wiping again.

"Can you go check on the customers, please? I have to grab my extra vest from the car."

"How'd they get in if we're not open?"

"They both walked in with their noses plugged up. Drove down from D.C. after visiting the monuments. Supposedly only came down here to visit The Pit after reading online reviews about our Sunday brunch. An hour's hike from D.C. to C-W because of traffic and the gift of a nosebleed for their first time crossing our county line. Why would I punish them for being fifteen minutes early when I can just get on you for being fifteen minutes late?" she said, finally cracking a smile and giving up on the stain. The smile faded quickly. "Everything okay, Zander? You look exhausted."

"Yeah, I'm fine. Just staying up editing videos later than I should. A keyboard has become my pillow."

"Let me know if you need a break."

"I'll be okay. Hey, remember my cousin is starting today. I'll get her up to speed in no time. You won't even notice if I disappear."

"I did put her on the schedule today. I hope you're right, though, so I can fire you the next time you're late." Bianca said, the smile slightly returning as she walked toward the front entrance.

Zander chuckled and shook his head. "I'll be sure to leave a good impression on our first-timers and the new bartender."

"I know you will, Zander. Thanks," Bianca said, passing through the curtain. Zander went his separate way toward the back room in the kitchen to get ready for the day ahead.

The lone couple in the corner was an older pair. They engaged Zander in a conversation about their two children who were long gone from their household and the vacations they'd been on since the beginning of the summer to Chile, Argentina, and Rome. They actually impressed Zander—it was only the second week of June. During the small talk, Zander could finally take their orders only after they inquired about each of The Pit's fifty-two drink specials.

Zander wasted time liking pictures on social media while the couple's food was prepared. He couldn't fake a smile for another long-winded conversation, so he hoped some pixilated tits would at least give him a smirk.

Scroll

Like

Scroll

Like

Scroll

Like

Scroll

Like

Scr—

Ten minutes went by without a flinch. Zander's thumb was getting Olympic-level training while he scrolled, but it was his eyes that strained and fell to fatigue first. He stopped at a photo of a woman in a white bikini with her back turned to the camera as she stared off into a sun-reflecting lake. The white of the bikini outlining the woman's ass and the angle of the sun in the water was enough to make Zander's eyes water. He set his phone on the counter and dried his face.

"You'll go blind if you hold that thing any closer next time," Kyle stated as he walked up to Zander, who was sitting next to his employee locker.

"Was it that bad?"

"Yeah, dude. Looked like you were trying to jump into your phone."

Zander considered this as he remembered how close his nose was to the screen, even more so when his reflection failed to come into focus as he dried his leaking eyes in the mirror.

"I'm running on four hours of sleep, man. Been pulling late nights and early mornings editing the videos I shot last week."

"Shit, that fight you set up at Chipotle was wild. They didn't hit you with destruction of property for breaking that table outside?"

Zander laughed under his breath as he tossed the napkin with his eye fluids in the trash. "Thanks, man, but no charges. Only a million views to help keep the channel growing. My next few videos should put me on the country's radar and keep me from being just a Cardinal-Wood icon. Helps that I have this sexy as fuck lead actress I've been scripting fights for. Ex-lover versus new lover's girlfriend, 'Clean-up in aisle six'—the Target rumble—and 'Excuse me, I ordered the sandwich, not the wrap'—the Eden Gardens Royale. The world can't get enough eye candy and she's the whole store. I'll get two million views just off her face alone."

"Damn, dude, you got a ring for her yet?"

"Fuck off."

"At least let me see a pic."

"Don't have one."

"Let me see her Insta, then."

"She doesn't have any social media accounts."

"The hell is her problem? She the only human without a brand to promote?"

"She says her life can't be contained in a screen."

Kyle made a face as if he was going to throw up, a dry heave with no sound.

"Alright, man, if you're back here fucking around, who's watching the front door?" Zander said, walking past Kyle on his way into the main section of the kitchen.

"Don't worry about that. I gave your cousin her first assignment as a new employee." Kyle said, smiling. "Told her to wait up there while I found you. No offense, man, but your cousin is kinda cute. She single?" he asked in a drawn-out, playful tone as he followed Zander out of the employee locker room.

"I doubt you're her type."

"That a challenge?"

"It's not supposed to be. Look. You know how this place can be for new-comers. Give her some space or I won't be able to protect you when she rips your head off."

"I'll take that as a challenge. I have an extra room at my spot she could move into, to save her the embarrassment of moving back in with her pops."

"Cardinal-Wood is full of one-bedroom apartments; don't think it will take long for her to find one for herself."

"How old is she, thirty? She looks thirty."

"Twenty-six."

Zander went to fill up two glasses of water for his first table as Kyle stood beside him.

"Challenge accepted."

Zander let out a laugh as he poured the last drink. "Alright, don't get your feelings hurt." The elderly couple joined in with a chuckle. "You'll be lucky if she hasn't already labeled you a creep." The two walked around the dining area to pro-vide water to another table of early guests, this time a party of five. Kyle stood back, glancing toward the host's podium. The silhouette of a woman leaning against the carved wooden stand caught his attention. The shadows surrounded her like she had arrived at a black carpet event, putting her figure on display.

Kyle had shown no boundaries with women during the three years Zander had known him. He had seen Kyle stop just short of harassing any woman over twenty-one who walked through the door. The first step was asking their age. Then there were the women he actually saw Kyle with in town. One ate the croutons out of her salad with her hands, another shaved her armpits every six months, and the most recent outing featured a headlining performance by the woman in front of her phone. She took a photo every twenty paces or ten minutes, attempting to break into the influencer scene.

"Take your shot, king. I'm interested to see if she entertains you," Zander said as he reached the table of the first guests of the morning. He poured the couple their refills as Kyle stood to the side, glancing periodically over toward the podium.

Without warning or hesitation, Kyle sped away power walking, already halfway back to his post by the time Zander was pouring the second drink. Zander noticed Bianca weaving around the tables, making her way to the podium, where an unfamiliar female currently stood.

"Hey, I'm back!" Kyle called out to the woman behind the podium, just as Bianca reached her at the same time. Neither Bianca nor the stranger turned around but kept their focus on the napkin on which Kyle was drawing a masterpiece. The short, black, thick curls of the new employee bounced as she shook her head from side to side.

"I've been trying to figure out what it means for the past ten minutes."

"Ten minutes?" Bianca asked, with a crack in her voice.

"Hey, Bianca. I just left to tell Zander his cousin is here," Kyle said, cutting in and finally getting the two spectators to turn around.

"You disappear for ten minutes, but not before you had time to draw this," Bianca said, letting the napkin unfold from her hand. The napkin revealed a basic sketch of a man in a red-and-blue cloak kneeling with seven swords poking from his back. "You don't have time to work on your dreams on my dime, Picasso."

"I was early enough to get that sketch done before we officially opened, thank you very much," Kyle said, tugging the sketch out of Bianca's hand in a way that it wouldn't rip. "I had an idea for a piece I could submit once I got in and had to get it out real quick."

Bianca's mouth tightened, causing her nose to flare up. "I hope you keep that motivation for the job I'm actually paying you for while I'm gone on vacation." Bianca turned to Julia. "I'm sorry. He thought leaving a new person at the front wasn't the same as leaving no one up here. It was nice meeting you, Julia, and welcome to the team. I apologize I can't stay and get to know you but I have to make sure the rest of this place is good to go. The brunch wave comes fast and strong."

"Thanks for having me," Julia waved with a smile as Bianca walked back toward the kitchen. She passed Zander on the way, who was holding a pitcher of water in his hand but his arms open wide, ready to embrace his cousin.

Once the initial greetings concluded, Kyle retook his post at the podium and Zander took Julia to the dining area. Zander gave his cousin the do's and don'ts of working at The Pit. He listed the fifty-two drink specials she'd have to memorize, one for each week of the year. Sunday brunch featured them all. He mentioned which employees were safe to talk to and the ones she should just nod to and keep it moving ("Bobby Velle, aka BO Bobby, can talk your ears off with explosive breath and even more offensive body odor. Stay clear."). He concluded with the boss, Bianca, like most employee-to-employee introductions do on the first day on the job, but didn't get past "don't get fooled by her smile" before pausing at the sight of a drop of blood running out of Julia's nose.

"Here, take this." Zander passed Julia a napkin from his apron. "I can't believe you haven't visited here once or that Uncle Quincy never brought you here himself. We always came to visit y'all: Hawaii, Japan—Germany was the shit."

Julia took the napkin and wiped away all traces of blood. "The most I saw him was during those mini family reunions. He never spoke highly about this place and, whenever I asked him why we didn't visit, he would just say I'd get the chance when I was older. And here I am as foretold by the modern-day prophet, my father."

"Yeah, well, as a Cardinal-Wood native, he should've warned you about the nosebleeds."

"He gave me some cotton plugs and told me to keep them close. Nothing else. I forgot them in the kitchen on my way here." Julia threw the used napkin in the trash behind the bar. "Dad or Google couldn't answer my question of why my nostrils are releasing rivers of blood suddenly. Maybe you can."

Zander chuckled. "Someone knows why but they aren't talking. What's known to everyone born and raised here is that all who cross the county line have to tough it out for three days until the nosebleeds stop. Three days until you breathe fresh air."

"Saw that online. Hearing it from you doesn't make it any easier to believe."

"You don't have to believe me now. Tomorrow is your third day here. You'll find out for yourself."

Zander pulled out his phone and squinted as he checked the time.

"Need glasses?"

"I need some sleep but I won't be getting that anytime soon." Zander paused as his exhausted mind struggled with what it was about to say. "I apologize, Jules, but I switched shifts with you."

"Excuse me, what now?"

"Had to convince Bianca to let me switch with you. I have to finish editing a video tonight and staying here until closing was going to get in the way. This new video needs to drop tomorrow."

"I have to close on my first day?"

"Consider it a favor for getting a job without an interview."

Julia considered this blessing her cousin was referring to as a sign of how far she was from where she wanted to be—not one that was getting her closer to where she wanted to go. After eight years of schooling, saying one-liners after examining a dead body like her childhood hero, Horatio Caine, was the next rung on her life ladder. Instead, she was picking up the afternoon-until-close shift for her younger cousin. Bartending had gotten her through Spellman while getting her master's and had allowed her to keep minor change in her pockets while school debt ate away (and still did) at whatever extra she tried to put in them. Bartending in a strange county at twenty-six and moving in with her father, who had been at sea more than he had been home during her first eighteen years of life, was not how she had planned to spend this time as she slowly inched toward the prime of her life.

The brunch rush came, and The Pit hit maximum capacity before noon. Servers on staff that day whizzed and zigzagged past each other like wide receivers running routes on the dining floor. The two cousins floated around at a slower pace as Zander continued to train Julia throughout the day. Considering her experience, it wasn't hard learning most of the drink specials. They had only gone over thirty out of the fifty-two, which Julia had written in her personal mini-notepad to memorize later. As Zander continued to review the list of drinks, Julia's attention drifted to the customers' conversations.

"Told my mom if she moved up here, it would heal her knee in no time. The water's *that* good," a woman at table six told her husband, who didn't look too pleased at the thought of his mother-in-law moving in.

Table ten, "You wouldn't believe it, Jan. I forgot to have the Jefferson kid stop by the house and water the plants. They went without water for two weeks while I was skiing. I came back and they had actually grown more without water."

"I told you some routines aren't necessary anymore."

Table fifteen, "I'm telling you, bro, she fucking disappeared. I flew her in for Memorial Day weekend and, while I was getting my rocks off before taking her to the airport that Monday evening, she disappeared when I was wiping sweat out of my eyes. I was stuck between a heart attack and trying to finish myself off until she called and blasted me about mailing her the things she brought on the trip. Then I saw her on IG live explaining to sixteen people watching how she teleported halfway around the country. There's—."

"Julia! What do you add next?"

"Huh?"

"What comes next in the Triple Wave after the Patron? Please tell me you were paying attention. I can't leave without you knowing a little something."

"You should've thought about that before throwing me under the bus on my first day."

Zander didn't flinch.

"A shot of rum and pineapple juice." Julia tucked the already closed notebook into her newly acquired vest all employees of The Pit sported.

"Thank you. You'll be able to halfway hold your own until the end of your shift," Zander said, squinting for the time again on his phone.

"You mean yours," Julia mumbled under her breath as she noticed her cousin struggling once again to see as he ignored another one of her snarky remarks. "Try to get some rest before you edit tonight. You might actually get some work done."

"Can't. My new lead actress is meeting me at my place and we are going to go over some scripts while I finish editing. No rest for the visionary."

"Just don't burn yourself out."

"I've been dropping three videos a week for an entire month. My subscribers have been jumping by the thousands daily. I think I'll only stop once I burn out, honestly. Have to ride this wave as long as it lasts."

Julia wasn't a stranger to Zander's success as a YouTuber. He had solicited his channel to her when she had called him about jobs in the area. Scripted fights weren't her thing so the subscribe button went untouched. He and his cast of a few like minds had close to a million subscribers and, judging by the look of Cardinal-Wood above from a plane, a significant portion of those followers could be in this county alone. Most rockets keep going until they reach a new world or the space in between. She could see why he had no intentions of slowing down.

Hours passed and evening came. The rush dwindled but patrons still filled The Pit. Shadowing her cousin behind the bar, having a stalled-out rocket ship of her own, limited Julia to using the tools in her arsenal—specifically the tools she had paid for but the return on investment hadn't cashed in yet. She used the time between orders to prematurely diagnose customers based on their drinks:

1. Long Island ice teas with depression

2.  Any vodka drink with narcissism

3.  Bourbon on the rocks with sociopathy

4.  Tequila shots with bipolar disorder

It didn't hurt to dream of using her skills accurately to one day to help make someone's world a better place. Tragedy strikes and there's usually a murderer, rapist, thief, or a force of nature on the other side of it. She had the knowledge to stop the first three and maybe a prayer could stop the last one. She knew she had what it takes to make one person's life change after a tragedy, a way to live after death. It's what she wished someone had done for her.

"Alright, time for me to get out of here," Zander said, passing a customer a shot of tequila. "Follow me."

The cousins found Bianca by the podium, giving Kyle what looked like stern instructions. She was using a wide range of hand motions to get her point across. Kyle's head went back and forth like a life-sized bobblehead, attempting to acknowledge whatever Bianca was saying.

"Don't forget to take the pictures down and wipe behind them too. Get Bobby and the new girl to take care of that while you and the others focus on the ceiling and tables. Oh, hello, new girl and the cousin who threw her under the bus on her first day."

"Come on, Bianca, I just got her off my back. Don't reactivate her, please."

"No, please remind him of his less-than-honorable ways," Julia said, giving Zander a nudge and a side eye.

"I try every chance I get. Zander, can you get Bobby before you head out? I don't have time to repeat myself. My flight is in the morning and I have to finish packing." Zander's eyebrows lifted and his eyes followed them like a flag being pulled up a post slowly. Bianca reiterated her request by saying they needed Bobby before Zander could leave, as Julia was going to finish the day shadowing him. Zander went on his search but not with the speed of someone excited to do it.

"Where are you heading to?" Julia asked during the break in the evening's instructions.

"Egypt. This vacation has been on the calendar for six months and I'm still trying to figure out if I will do everything I planned while I'm there."

"How long are you going for?"

"Three weeks. Just under a month to explore ancient history and visit one of the old seven wonders of the world."

"Old?"

"Yeah. Would you believe it's not listed as one of the new, modern seven wonders of the world? They've been put into a legacy program, forgotten by this new age. Better visit soon before someone tears them down for a resort."

Kyle cut in. "You know you can extend your trip. See all the sites you want, start a petition, and spread the news about the atrocities society is committing to history. We'll take care of The Pit for you."

"You wish—" Bianca said but her words trailed over the same mental cliff over which her thoughts had fallen.

Suddenly the rich smell of whiskey and wood polish that filled The Pit faded away, displaced by an aroma that started off as lavender in the nose but incited the taste of honey on the tongue. It overtook the owner and the two employees followed each other down the newly found mind-fall mountain. The intoxicating odor put to shame every aisle at Bath & Body Works known to man—or at least to those three—and they continued to fall. The descent took them past every anxiety put in the hands of the creator, held on the back of the owner, stuck on the mind of a stranger... and they landed on a voice.

"Hello, is Zander Thurman in?" the voice asked, soothing the space in the brain where pleasure lives. The sound was soft and comforting, ringing with the pitch of a tuning fork as it set and configured images in the minds of those who listened. Bianca felt the solace of a lone cloud on a summer day and Kyle felt a warm blanket in front of a fire on a winter night. An image of an enclosed coffin flashed in Julia's mind. She was unable to shake the feeling she was still falling.

Standing by the front entrance was a woman with black locs flowing from her head to her shoulders. She wore a tailored black suit and the demeanor of a lawyer who just won a tough case or a parishioner elated after hearing a heartfelt sermon. Her smile was too wide for her to have come from a funeral unless it represented relief at the death of the deceased. She waited for a response. The possibility of the door not opening and the impossibility of the guest standing there crossed Julia's mind but the thought was fleeting. As the woman moved closer Julia was captivated by her beauty and her locs, which made an unnatural movement, as if they were shifting side to side on their own. Bianca and Kyle, mesmerized just the same, turned to greet the guest, mimicking Julia's speechless manner.

The woman's presence—not her height—grew as she floated toward the podium. Standing at five foot five, just under Julia's line of sight, the woman was illuminated by a force from her pores, possibly the perfume she was wearing, but Julia didn't mind the overexposure. The smell was inviting; Julia felt herself take a step closer as if she was going to greet the guest instead of answer her question.

Bianca's brain finished resetting, allowing her to respond first. "H- Hello. He's in the back locating an employee for me. How can I help you?"

"We have an appointment this evening. It seems too early for him to be home, so I thought I could catch him here. May I see a menu while I wait?"

Kyle reached for a menu out of a stack placed on the side of the podium. "You must be the actress he hired for his skits he's about to shoot. I'm Kyl—"

"Kyle." The woman finished for him, pointing to the left side of her chest with a smile, indicating his name tag. Her wide smile returned, sporting teeth that reflected the light. It was playful but somehow looked like the grin of a shark. Sweat built up on Kyle's forehead as the woman reached for the menu, which Julia thought unusual until she noticed her own brow perspire. "Yes, I'm Libby Yolke, the new lead on the Hearts & Bones YouTube channel." She took a half bow. "Nice to meet you, Kyle, and you as well, Bianca. And who might you be?" Libby asked, turning her attention to Julia.

There was a glimmer in Libby's eyes as if they held a distant star. Julia didn't notice this flickering light until their eyes met. The flash was brief but long enough to freeze Julia's own name on the tip of her tongue until the shimmer died down.

"Julia. It's m-my first day."

"Ah, no name tag for newbies. Nice to meet you, Julia," Libby said, sending another ping of a tuning fork ringing between Julia's ears at the sound of her own name. Libby looked over the menu as the three continued to watch. "Wow, fifty-two drink specials! I would say today is my lucky day, but there's so many options and not enough time to decide."

"Hey, Libby!" Zander called out as he walked up to the podium with Bobby trailing him. "I thought you were going to meet me at my place."

"Wasn't sure you'd get off by 7:30, so I came here instead. Glad I did or I wouldn't have met your lovely coworkers." Libby closed the menu and scanned the lineup of The Pit employees and Bianca. Zander easily broke the ranks and proceeded toward Libby, giving her a hug. Bobby, who was shorter than Kyle but built with the frame of a Mini Cooper, took his place in the viewing gallery on Julia's right side. Sweat immediately spilled from his acne-filled pores.

"Damn, she's beautiful," Kyle said under his breath, loud enough for Julia to hear with Bianca between them. It was maybe loud enough for Libby to hear too, but that didn't matter. Her focus was on Zander, whose face mimicked the electricity illuminating from Libby like a lightning rod after being struck. Able to sway past the lavender scent that filled the waiting area, the voice that spoke to the mind, and the looks that bound the others in place with a heat wave, the energy that had escaped Zander most of the day returned.

Bobby attempted to speak but couldn't form his words fast enough. "She's—."

"Here, hold this for me, Bobby, my love." Libby passed him the menu.

"Alright, Julia. I'll see you tomorrow afternoon and try not to work too hard." Zander said playfully. Julia responded with a half smile and a wave, unable to reciprocate the charm.

"Goodbye, it was nice meeting you all. Can't wait to come back for the drink specials," Libby said as she and Zander exited the building, taking the heat with them.

Title: "Excuse Me, I Ordered the Sandwich, Not the Wrap": The Eden Gardens Royale

(Skit rough draft)

Music starts.

OPEN ON EXTERIOR: EDEN GARDENS PARK—DAY

The Eden Gardens park entrance sign. Focus on the sculpted copper snake coiled around the rainbow structure's left pillar. Zoom out to a full shot of the gold lettering arched over the visitors as they cross into the manicured tree tunnel.

CUT TO Inside the Park

Families and individuals, young and old, enjoy themselves in the lush green paradise. People walk along the trails carved into the grounds and couples sit around the Eternity Fountain eating meals from one of the area food trucks as a marbled angel statue with a helmet, shield, and extended wings watches from the center.

CUT TO A single food truck, El Bocado, and its line of patrons

Zander stands in line waiting to place an order (mic'd up for live audio). He places his order for a chicken wrap in real time.

CUT TO David (cast) working at the food truck for the day for paid promotion

CUT TO Libby yolke walking in the crowd heading toward El Bocado

Libby's blonde hair rocks with every move she takes against the wind and her green eyes reflect the sun. She proceeds forward, each step more fierce than the last. As she stands head and shoulders above most, she can see all the necks that snap in her direction. The bikini top cupping her God-given treasures ensure any lost eyes follow her along the way. Distressed denim shorts exposing her curves freeze any soccer mom in the area.

CUT TO El Bocado

David calls Zander's order number but Libby gets to the window first.

Libby: Excuse me, I ordered the sandwich, not the wrap.

David, stunned by her beauty, doesn't object even though he glances at Zander behind her.

David: I apologize, miss. Take the wrap for later and we'll have your sandwich right out.

Zander: Yo, that's my order!

David: Sir—.

"So what do you think?" Zander blurted out to Libby as she reviewed the script he had just given her.

Sitting in the designated office of his two-bedroom apartment, Zander placed his feet on top of the wheels of his computer chair and leaned in to better hear the hasty response. They were two hours into their editing session and he couldn't wait three minutes before picking Libby's brain. She had been helpful most of the night, whispering in his ear about what scenes to cut and what music to add, raising the temperature in the room after each suggestion. Zander thought the feeling was mutual as sweat built up over his brow as the night progressed and Libby's green eyes briefly flashed with passing light like a comet shooting across both pupils as the last edit of the skit was completed. Compelled to give her his newest piece of work, Zander knew restraining from hearing her voice pierce the silence wasn't an option.

Libby's blonde hair shifted from one shoulder to the other with a tilt of her head as she placed the script by her side. For a moment Zander thought he saw a few strands (or maybe those were hands?) lunging toward him, stretching across the coffee table from her seat on the futon. Zander rubbed his eye and carried his hand up to his forehead to wipe away a bead of sweat. The clouds that had slowly covered his vision throughout the day had finally turned into a blinding thunderstorm and Libby was the lighthouse guiding him forward. He remembered the rest Julia said he should get and still noted it as a goal not worth taking.

Libby's eyes flashed with the light of a seductive star before turning back to green. "The script is amazing! A few edits and we'll have something cooking," she said with a grin only shared between sharks and the guests that roam their seas. The storm in Zander's eyes cleared just enough to see Libby and all her beauty. Rest would have to wait.

The last few hours of Julia's shift were a combination of pure ecstasy and a terrible hangover. Between taking drink orders as she shadowed Bobby and the body odor her cousin had warned her about—laced with a mix of sweat, onions, and Axe body spray—she found her memory holding onto the scent of lavender that had filled the waiting area when Libby entered. Julia couldn't evict the image of Libby's mystically divine face that had moved into its own corner in her mind. The black locks that flowed from Libby's scalp, her skin that reflected the light, and her green eyes took Julia further inside her own head and produced a kaleidoscope of feelings. Even though that was Julia's first time seeing Libby, in her head and creeping down toward her heart, she felt as if they had been longtime friends, maybe inseparable or romantically involved and now distant lovers.

Not only had the exotic lavender scent revealed the face of Libby Yolke with a connected past, but the periodic taste of honey on Julia's tongue accompanying it revealed a future that Julia didn't think possible, one she gave up dreaming long ago.

"Can we have our dessert to go, please?" a mother asked, sitting with her family of four—two kids no older than twelve, stuck on their phones, and two parents ready to go. The chasm in Julia's gut widened as she willed her mind to focus on writing the mother's order instead of holding on to the image of a beautiful face filled with promise anchored there.

Bobby clasped his hands and rubbed them together to dry the sweat glistening in his palms. "No problem, ma'am. And what would y'all like this evening?" he asked, moving his hand up to reposition his matted-down hair. The blonde shag he had started the day with had morphed into a replica of a dirty mop as sweat gradually leaked from his scalp. In that moment of swiping his hair, the dam holding back the smell of his underarms fell, smacking the mother sitting next to him with the first wave. The mother's nose scrunched up in a way that wasn't polite or inconspicuous. She closed her eyes as if shards of smell were about to pierce them.

The woman flung her hands in the air and stood up from the table. "I'll be in the car, Jim," she said as she stormed toward the exit, tossing her green purse over her shoulder.

Bobby's pudgy face blushed a bright red, turning his head into the king zit amongst the acne that peppered his cheeks. Jim paused briefly. Julia couldn't tell if it was out of embarrassment at his wife's reaction until she heard a gag from him and both kids looked up from their phones with faces of disgust that matched their mother's. Then the odor from Bobby's sweat-stained shirt reached Julia's nostrils. The smell of sweat, onions, and the whiskey wood of The Pit gave Julia the impression of a junkyard fire.

"I'll take the check instead."

"We'll get that right out to you, sir." Julia tried to hold a professional face as long as possible before making her way toward the register. Bobby's musk wasn't enough to loosen the anchor Libby's lavender scent had placed in her mind any more than the tasks of the job, but the taste of honey on her tongue intensified whenever her focus drifted away from the smile that festered in her head, leaving Julia feeling robbed of a pleasure she was finding hard to explain. She would have to dwell on it later as Bobby trailed her to the register, pulling her thoughts back to The Pit with each step.

"I-I'm not like this on purpose, you know. I mean, I apologize for the smell. It's a condition," Bobby said, losing breath between each word as he kept pace with Julia. "I already changed into the spare shirt I brought today. Maybe I should bring—."

"It's okay, Bobby. I understand," Julia said as she reached the register. Even though she had no experience of profusely sweating or smelling like molded tuna in the workplace, she didn't mind comforting him. She stepped to the side as Bobby accessed the register to retrieve the family's ticket. "What's the condition called?" Julia asked, tightening her face as she noticed drops of sweat left behind on the register's touch screen.

Stopping to wipe his hands on the seam of his pants, Bobby went back to punching buttons on the screen. "It's called hyperhidrosis. Bianca usually has me in the kitchen toward the end of my shift. But since your cousin has better things to do, and she has her head in her ass because of her trip, I'm out here helping you." A final wet squish of the screen produced a receipt bound to have a moist imprint from the fingertips reaching for it. "I'm sorry; it's not your fault," Bobby said, turning to face Julia. She could now see the exhaustion of the day pushing down on his eyes. "Past couple hours have been dragging. I feel like shit and I'm ready to go home."

As they went to hand the father his check, Julia could comprehend that feeling fully and felt validated to know the sensation wasn't exclusive to her. Now that her eyes were out of her own head, Julia could notice the others who had locked pupils with Libby Yolke became bogged down in the quicksand of their own minds as well.

Bianca's head was further from where Bobby said it was. At fifteen minutes to closing, she was still in the building. She wasn't in a rush to pack her things and leave like she had been hours ago, as she stood by the front windows near the podium staring outside with a frozen glare. Julia got the sense Bianca didn't want to leave at all. Bianca looked more like a dog waiting for her owner to come home.

Uninterested in the woman with the green purse giving her an earful, no doubt about Bobby, Bianca switched from her overbearing older sister-manager act into the role of an absent mother as she nodded and waved the woman off.

Behind Bianca, ignoring the appeals of the disturbed mother and his boss in front of him, Kyle hunched over the podium, scribbling on a pile of napkins. His broad shoulders acted like a wall shielding his work from the handful of guests and servers who filled the dining area. The mother violated by Bobby's BO finished her closing arguments without a response from Bianca and stormed out of the building.

A lavender aroma rested on Julia's nostrils, bringing back that image of Libby's face in her head. The bright smile blinded her mind's eye. She glanced around the dining area to see if the woman with looks just short of a goddess had returned, only to see Bobby cleaning off the table used by the last family they had served.

"Libby's perfume's been stuck in my nose since she showed up." Julia spoke out loud, reasoning with herself and rubbing her nose, hoping to dissipate the unwanted particles.

Bianca turned away from the window, focusing on Julia and Bobby as if an invisible antenna connected to her brain had picked up an alert. Bypassing the doodling host in front of her, she made her way toward the two with a speed that matched the version of Bianca Julia had met earlier that day.

"Who?" Bobby stopped to ask with a stack of dirty plates in front of him.

"Libby Yolke. She left with my cousin earlier. Remember?"

"I haven't been able to get that name or face out of my head since *he* left. Why'd you say *woman* though?" he asked, trapping sweat between the creases of his perplexed face.

Bianca cut in with an executive statement a few paces away from the table. "Bobby, take those plates to the back and help the cooks clean the kitchen."

Bobby looked over his shoulder at the owner of the establishment hovering behind with her arms on her waist and then turned back toward Julia with a shrug.

"Duty calls, new girl." He hoisted up the plates, eager to carry them back to his sanctuary known as the kitchen.

Bianca looked at Julia with a smile a Management 101 conference would promote or a porcelain doll would wear. "Hope you enjoyed your first day. You can head home now. Just come ready to work tomorrow. It's going to be another busy day."

Many years of "first days" because of her father's military career had taught Julia it was best to observe and not disrupt any established norms. Not refusing a generous offer to go home a few minutes early from work was somewhere on her list of life lessons, so she accepted without hesitation. It had been a long day and the smile glued onto Bianca's face, the whites of her teeth, appeared to get brighter, similar to Libby's grin that had taken residence in Julia's mind for the past two hours.

Julia scratched her right temple. "Thanks for letting me work here. I really appreciate it."

"Zander spoke highly of you. Just live up to it so I don't regret it. See you tomorrow."

Julia nodded and made her way to the exit. She removed her vest and placed it over her arm as she walked past Kyle, who was still focused on his stack of napkins, which looked like a collage of mini portraits. She didn't bother to look closely at the colorful faces, just pressed on toward the door. She didn't even wonder why Bianca had hinted at being at work the next day instead of being gone for her trip. The only thing on Julia's mind was Libby Yolke and sleep.

The morning sun peeked through the white-lace blinds covering Julia's bedroom window. Light knocking on her sealed eyelids gradually turned the darkness she was seeing in her dreams into a reddish hue until her eyes opened, ready to greet the new day. If the sun's rays hadn't wakened her, the smell of bacon and cinnamon pancakes coming from the kitchen would have tugged her out of bed eventually.

Her mother's cooking was on Julia's mind during her time away from home, allowing the enticing smell to hook onto her nose and carry her downstairs.

Gunshots blasted from the living room TV. Julia's mother sat in the room, which was to the left of the open kitchen. The only thing separating the furniture from the appliances was the wood floor on one side and tile on the other. With her eyes glued to the screen, Marie Thurman took a sip out of a martini glass placed on the coffee table to her right. Julia reached the bottom of the stairs and was greeted by a plate on the wood dining table with two pancakes with cinnamon swirls ingrained, three strips of bacon, and scrambled eggs with cheese still melting on and over onto the plate.

"Good morning, sugar pie. I made you some breakfast. Get your plate and come sit. Our show is on." Marie said, turning her attention toward her daughter. Her natural black twists of hair bounced around the sculpted cheeks they hung over as she patted the seat intended for Julia.

A sense of déjà vu came over Julia as she studied her mother's beauty momentarily. Marie was cozy on the couch in a grey sweatshirt with blue letters spelling out the letters of her alma mater, Hampton University. Had Julia lived this day before? If not, the life in her mother's eyes could have trapped her in this moment forever. She retrieved her plate and took a seat next to her mother.

"Urban Hell-Raisers." That was the name of the *CSI: Miami* episode on TV. It wasn't Julia's favorite episode, just one she remembered. Disguised armed robbers stormed a bank, one of whom wore a red *hannya* mask. Machine guns blazing, the red-faced demon killed a teller before fleeing but lost a partner in just the same way to the Miami PD. Standing over the dead robber after the chaos, Horatio Caine could respond only with a classic one-liner. *"Miami has a new breed of criminal,"* Horatio said, putting on his sunglasses. The screen cut to the opening credits and Julia took a bite of cinnamon-laced pancakes drenched in syrup, sending a jolt to her brain that attempted to lock her in this moment forever.

"Let's stay in and finish season four today. I have nothing planned. Whatcha think?" Marie asked, taking another sip from her martini glass. A mole under her left eye disappeared in the creases of her smile as she set her cup back on the coffee table.

Before Julia could answer, the clanking of ice from the martini glass grew louder than the sounds coming from the TV. Each ricochet of the cubes produced a sound of cracking glass that pierced the eardrums and slowed time itself. The face before Julia, resembling Maria, melted away with pieces of skin falling like raindrops onto her Hampton University sweater, slowly revealing the face of Libby Yolke. The black mini twists of Marie Thurman's hair transformed into the flowing locks Julia had seen the day before. Amber eyes, with a burning glow, replaced the brown cornerstone of her mother's spirit.

Time stopped. The ice cubes in the martini glass locked into place, trapped in the hands of the Libby–Marie hybrid just inches above the coffee table. Julia could still hear glass cracking as if Barry Bonds was taking a sledgehammer to a windshield and was two hits away from giving in. Unbound in this frozen space, Julia kept her eyes on Libby as the flesh that substituted for her mother's, which rivaled the glow of the sun, dripped away as well. Pieces of skin melted past a widening smile as all of Libby's teeth sharpened to a point in a predator's grin.

Libby's facade fell completely from the left side while the right was slowly losing its human form. What Julia saw underneath resembled not a woman, but a monster. The grey skin looked rigid and dry with cracks or like the scales of an alligator. While the right eye still had a humanlike amber iris, the left had undergone a complete transformation. The white of the sclera had been dyed black, removing the iris and pupil, which were displaced by what Julia could compare only to a distant star she's seen in the night sky. Locks on Libby's left side disappeared, leaving behind a round scalp with more grey scales. Above hovered seven gold needles like a crown over the monster's head.

The crackling of invisible glass continued until *bang!* Julia's vision cracked. The image of the monster known as Libby Yolke and the surrounding room split into thousands of pieces, disturbing the view like a cracked window. Julia focused on the half-formed sinister grin between the cracks of this fractured lens. With razor-sharp teeth that looked manicured for Shark Week, Julia wondered what they were made to eat before the room enclosed in stained glass shattered, ending her nightmare.

Julia's eyes opened, not to a sunny day, but to grey skies and rain beating against her bedroom window. And Marie wasn't cooking downstairs. She was dead. Julia woke up with a nosebleed, which was hopefully her last, and a question: why was Libby Yolke in her head?

The sound of cracking glass from her nightmare continued in tune with the rain thumping against the window, dwindling to a murmur in Julia's spirit to a place where her natural ears couldn't hear. The sounds grew soft like creeping footsteps in iced-over snow. She would have to wait for the answer she was looking for to have her world shatter again.

2

## GOD IN CODE

Blood trickled down two lanes of red leading out of Julia's nostrils, dripping onto her mother's grey Hampton University sweater Julia had worn to bed the night before. *Fuck.* Julia watched as the spattered blood seeped into the sweatshirt she'd kept stainless for the past eight years. Another drop fell and added itself to the botched tie-dye job. Julia shifted her body to get out of bed. Tilting her head back, Julia hoisted herself up, believing she had the energy a night's rest usually provided. Wobbly legs and weak knees revealed themselves and sent her tumbling to the floor. Sprinkles of blood, guided by gravity, fell on the carpet with more grace than was afforded to Julia.

Lifting her head from the floor, Julia watched as the tiny red spots of blood soaked into the carpet. Unpacked bags lined the surrounding walls. In the guest room of her father's house was no better symbol of claiming unfamiliar territory as your own than soiling the ground in blood. Bobby's clustered acne flashed in Julia's head as she watched the stains deepen.

The specs of blood on the carpet turned into Julia's very own connect-the-dot map for her memory as she sprawled in a lazy plank position. The association between Bobby and the stains on the floor, meaning more than the bumps on his face, hid itself as she strained to push herself off the ground. The weight on her shoulders now was familiar after the heaviness she experienced yesterday during her first day at The Pit, forcing herself through a long evening of taking orders and trying to hold on to a *fantasy* of her dead mother at the same time. It felt like a living dream, one she'd had many times but never so vivid. It was something Julia could actively experience between orders. Then Julia recalled the face lodged in her head guiding her toward that fantasy like a Peloton instructor—Libby Yolke, using *her* figure and charm to keep Julia yearning for more, peddling on some mental fitness bike chanting *"Don't quit!"* while a radio played in the background.

*"Why'd you say woman, though?"*

As Julia finally stood on her feet, Bobby's question rang in her ears. Her nightmare replayed on the mind-screen mounted in her brain. Rough grey scales covered the half-faced monster, revealing itself under her mother's flesh. A grin exposed sharp teeth embellished with a crown of floating gold spikes and star-like eyes that looked deep into Julia's soul, even now. *That wasn't all Bobby said, was it?* Like she was traveling under multiple overpasses on a highway, dark spots in her memory kept her from piecing the full day together.

The rain continued tapping against the window. Suddenly a cracking of glass snapped no louder than a whisper in Julia's spirit and she heard what she had overlooked the day before. *"I haven't been able to get that name or face out of my head since he left. Why'd you say woman, though?"*

*Since he left?* It was easy to assume Bobby meant when Zander left. Her thoughts were in a different place and arguing semantics on the first day on the job was an afterthought, never mind Bianca sending her home early. Watching her mother's face melt away in her nightmare transformed Bobby's words.

*Zander!*

Head tilted upward, Julia reached for her cell phone. Holding the phone toward the ceiling, keeping the remaining drops of blood at bay, she searched for Zander's contact info. Part of her felt like she was overreacting—maybe it was only a bad dream and she had nothing to worry about. The heart beating through her chest suggested otherwise. And the monster's celestial eyes haunting her headspace only encouraged her to press the call button faster. The dial tone rolled over for what felt like an infinite loop until there was silence on the other end.

"Hello? Zander?" Julia looked at her phone screen, verifying Zander had answered the call. Five seconds later she still had heard no response. "Hello—."

*Hey, this is Zander Thurman. Sorry I missed your call. If this is a business inquiry, email HeartsandBonesCEO@gmail.com or shoot me a text. If not, I'll get back to you when I can.*

Lacking the words to fill the space after the beep that followed every voicemail, this one acted like an exclamation point to an obnoxious call. Julia hung up the phone and decided a text would get through to Zander faster. It was 7:30 a.m. Zander had said he would be up late editing videos and reviewing scripts. He could still be asleep. Why disturb his rest over her nightmare?

Julia sent a text telling Zander to call her back when he woke up and tossed her phone onto the bed. She tiptoed around bags and boxes she'd been meaning to unpack since moving to town, ensuring no extra blood fell on her way out of the room and into the bathroom down the hall. Her bare feet pressed against the chilled hardwood floor. Minus the blood clogging her nose accompanied by the taste of iron running down her throat, Julia wished for the smell of cinnamon pancakes to creep through. That's all it was—a *wish*.

The cruel dream was just an expression of her heart, what she had wanted for years, even while her mother was still living. Marie Thurman had never once mentioned visiting her husband's childhood home. She had stopped making pancakes for two long before Julia went off to college. Some kind of tonic drink became Marie's first choice for a breakfast partner by the time Julia was eleven years old, meaning Marie left Julia to herself and a stash of frozen waffles while Marie drank the day away. She had had that dream tucked in her heart for a while now. Julia still wished like a child and last night was no different. A dream without the possibility of achievement is only a wish.

Julia wiped the blood off her lip and from the rim of her nostrils with a tissue. Convincing herself one last time she had only had a nightmare, she tossed the red glob into the toilet. Julia turned on the shower, deciding to get started with her morning. Getting back into bed to fall back asleep somehow felt like a risk not worth taking at the moment.

After showering, Julia changed into clothes matching the damp hours ahead. Zipping up the suitcase, she pulled her fit-of-the-day out, once again saving the final unpacking for a later date. She couldn't help but glance back over at her phone on the bed. The phone lay tauntingly next to her mother's stained sweatshirt on the bed with a blackened, lifeless screen. She had already checked, once she got out of the shower, whether Zander had texted her back. All she found out was the twenty-minute shower she thought she took was actually forty-five. Eight fifteen was still early and neither of them had to be at The Pit until two, another reason Zander could still be asleep. She knew no text had been sent between her getting dressed and repacking her bag with the clothes that hadn't made the day's cut because her phone was off vibrate during that time. Now all she could do was look at the phone and *will* a message to come through with some sort of techno-kinesis that only exists in comic books and movies.

A rumble worked its way around Julia's stomach. She placed a hand covering the screams of hunger coming from her body and looked at the black screen on the bed one last time before reaching for the phone and placing it in her pocket. *He'll call by the time I eat.* Julia left her mother's sweatshirt behind on the bed as she went downstairs.

"You ready to go?" Julia's father's voice called out from behind, freezing her midway down the wooded Loretto Cathedral cut staircase. Both of them were highlighted by silver rays piercing through the large, arched, front-facing window of the home.

"Yeah. I was about to go get some breakfast," Julia answered, partially facing Quincy Thurman. His brick-wall-like stature curved around her peripheral vision, almost bending him to full view.

"And leave me behind?" he asked, fastening a gold watch around his left wrist.

A joke about a dad leaving his family behind to chase his career crossed her mind, but more pressing matters pushed it aside. "I didn't know I had to send an invitation before leaving, plus I just needed some fresh air."

Quincy chuckled. "Last night, when you got home, I asked you to take me to work this morning because my car is in the shop. You agreed with no problem. You actually just waved me off and said, *'Yeah, sure,'* on your way upstairs."

Julia, now fully facing her father, tried to keep the confusion flaring up in her mind from showing up on her face. He was wearing a white dress shirt, unbuttoned at the neck with no tie, and blue slacks. The grey on his head resembled the clouds in the sky that morning. From where Julia stood, his glasses reflected the gloomy natural lighting coming from the giant window overlooking the staircase. Not grasping yesterday was becoming the theme of today, and being reminded of another blind spot just made her check her phone for a notification from Zander that she knew wasn't there.

"I heard you were already up so I didn't think I needed to remind you. Come on, you can grab something to eat on the way."

On the road in Julia's black Altima, Julia and Quincy joined the rest of the morning commuters under the rain covering Cardinal-Wood. Solar panels around C-W were amongst the many factors that had earned the area the title of "County-of-Tomorrow" from Forbes. From the rooftops of the houses in Quincy's neighborhood to the streetlights guarding the roads and even the side paneling of taller buildings breaking through the high tree line, the black solar cells were the foundation of the county, able to harness the energy from light above and bring down the sky itself on a stormy day. For a moment Julia thought she was driving in the sky, trapped in the clouds enclosed in the solar panel's reflective lenses.

A howl deep in Julia's stomach brought her back to earth. Stopped at a red light, Julia spotted a McDonald's just ahead and fell victim to the pleas from her gut. She was starving and now wasn't the time to be picky. A self-driving Uber with its lone backseat passenger to her right pulled ahead once the light changed. Julia cut behind it and turned into the drive-through.

Quincy looked up from his phone. "Another fifteen minutes and you could grab food at the cafeteria in my building. I didn't think this place was on your list of breakfast choices or else I would have told you sooner."

Julia's stomach reminded her once again of its emptiness as she pulled into the drive-through. "These McGriddles will be gone by the time I drop you off. Don't think I can wait another fifteen minutes."

"Fair enough." Quincy paused before asking, "I saw your mother's old sweatshirt on your bed before we left. How's it feel being fully acclimated to the Cardinal-Wood air?" His question was similar to "*Do you feel any older?*" which gets asked every birthday. A new year's wisdom rarely comes on the day of just as a strained back or brittle knees usually appear months down the line.

"I feel the same as yesterday and the day before that," Julia answered before saying her order over the intercom. "Just hope the random nosebleeds are really over," she added, thinking about the lie she just told. The fear rushing through her today was nonexistent yesterday. She wished to go back to the fabricated bliss from the day before. It was better than the emptiness brought on by an enlightened dream. Julia checked her phone once again for a notification from Zander she knew wasn't there.

"Your mom said the same thing after her third day here."

"She never mentioned coming here."

"That's because she never wanted to come back."

A wall of silence fell between the two as Julia pulled up to get her order from the next window. Julia reached for the food at the same time her mind reached back for a memory of her mother, back to a time when, as a kid, Julia was interested in her parents' backstory. This was before her mother added a second martini to her morning routine, probably because she was still driving Julia to school.

*"How'd you and Daddy meet?"* Julia remembered asking from the backseat of the family's green Dodge Stratus with her backpack resting between her hovering

feet. Marie's eyes, propped up by the bags underneath brought on by sleeplessness, locked onto Julia's from the rearview mirror. For a time Julia thought the deep black sacks under her mother's eyes were a brand of makeup only adults could wear. Not until Julia got older did she learn there was some truth to that thought.

*"I was on an academic field trip for my biology major. My class drove up to a magical place to collect samples of fruit and vegetables that the news reported had decomposed at a slower rate than any produce in the country and even around the world."* Marie stopped once she noticed the confusion on Julia's face. Tucking the answer into a full-length story wasn't what her daughter wanted. From Julia's perspective, her middle school mind was trying to understand. In between the half-truths parents tell their kids is always a lie. Now, Julia assumed it was a story her mother's heart was not ready to tell.

*"I passed out at a farmer's market and your father was there to pick me up,"* Marie finished. *"Go, have a great day. I'll tell you the rest once you get home from school. We can even get ice cream!"* she said, unlocking the car door in front of Julia's school. Julia got out of the car and went the rest of the day wondering what more there could be to the story. Once Julia got home later that day, though, Marie was too drunk to remember the conversation and ice cream was just a broken promise. Julia never again asked her mother how she met her father.

"Your destination is on your right. 17458 Axiom Dr. Cardinal-Wood, VA."

"You work here?" Julia asked around a mouthful of her second McGriddle, which added an obnoxious tone that was deserved, based on the sight in front of her.

Behind a gate and security checkpoint stood a tall, glass-clad structure built like a cathedral. The crystal chapel had blackened panels from top to bottom and two spires, one each at the far ends of the compound. Directly in the center of the building was a dome with a closed retractable roof, common only to observatories. On the front lawn of this architectural wonder a sculpture of a large, bronze hand cupping the world in its palm separated the foot traffic of people entering and leaving the building crafted by Cardinal-Wood's very own Wizard of Oz.

"I can show you better than I can tell you. Come in for a tour if you have some time." Quincy was more focused on the article he was reading on his phone than the obsidian castle in front of him.

Julia looked at her phone. It was a quarter past nine and still no text from Zander. A tour to feed her curiosity didn't sound so bad now that her hunger had subsided. The morning was dragging and she had time to kill.

Axiom Research Agency visitor!

Julia glanced down at the visitor badge she had just received.

"Appreciate it, Earl!" Quincy blurted out with a wave from the passenger seat.

Julia looked at the half smirk forming between Earl's pudgy cheeks that shifted the cap on his head as he pressed a button lifting the barrier to the gate.

"No problem, Mr. Q. Enjoy your day," Earl replied with a wave that was more gesture than pleasantry.

Julia observed the badge clipped over her heart one more time before driving forward. Based on Earl's previous instructions to get a visitor badge from the visitor center up the street before entering the main compound, the exclamation point at the end of *"visitor!"* was just as uninviting. It took some encouragement from Quincy and an exchange of personal information from Julia before receiving the credentials to pull ahead.

"I forgot my badge twice already and he's the only guard to help. Anyone else would've sent us to the visitor center to wait an hour in line."

"I guess it's my lucky day." Julia parked between two Teslas.

"Funny, but that badge would only get you through the front door and back outside if you weren't with me. You're going to get the real inside scoop now."

Julia had thought her father, a retired U.S. Navy chaplain, would find a job at a place of worship. There wasn't a cross in sight, a sailor in spiritual need, or a

Sister Johnson sporting her Sunday's best hat. It was Monday and everyone walking toward the building was carrying a briefcase and wearing a badge. Quincy clipped his onto his collar as the two approached the statue of the hand. The statue was colossal, as if its sculptors had styled the bust to mimic the hand of a giant. The Earth, large in its own way, looked like a snowball resting in its palm.

"You get it? He's got the whole world in his hands! Like the church rhyme," Quincy said as he noticed Julia stop to examine the work of art.

Julia looked over at her father with constricting eyebrows and back up at the sculpture as she wrapped her head around the thought that it was fashioned after God, not a mere giant. "I guess it is self-explanatory, huh?"

"You'd be surprised. The controversy that arises from most people outside these gates to even imagine that this is God's hand holding the world amazes me every day. But if we replaced the Earth with a cell phone and told people *"This is you!"* that might empower some of them to say they are gods. I mean, look at all the crap we can do with just a box in our hand these days."

Mass communication—one of those pieces of crap Quincy was referring to—and Zander's YouTube channel mixed in with other fecal matters of technological advancement came across Julia's mind. Had Zander uploaded his new video yet? Maybe that would let her know he was okay. She still could not understand why a dream would compel her to check on Zander, but she knew relief would come only with some sort of confirmation. She searched for the HeartsandBones channel on the YouTube app and pressed "Subscribe" when she got there. His last upload, titled "The Burrito Brawl," was four days ago. She almost unsubscribed from the channel at that moment but decided it would be easier to find the next time she needed it if she kept the subscription.

"Come on, baby girl, I have to get inside."

Julia followed Quincy to the front doors of the glass building positioned under gold letters implying its namesake—Axiom Research Agency. Quincy pressed his badge against a card reader at the entrance, which returned a beep loud enough to be heard over the rain drumming against the building and concrete.

Quincy pulled the door open and walked in. Julia tried to follow but he stopped her before she could get a foot inside. "Buzz in through the visitor entrance. I'll wait for you in The Circle," Quincy said, pointing to Julia's right.

She did not know what he meant by The Circle but figured she'd find out soon. A few paces to her right and she was underneath more gold lettering—Sp. Visitor's Entrance. Julia remembered Earl's warning that her visitor badge was good for only twenty-four hours before he scanned the barcode on the back and handed it to her. She placed that barcode on her badge against the card reader and it replied with an inviting tone, unlocking the door.

Inside, a white marble floor starkly contrasted with the black glass framing the building. A miniature sign attached to winding steel line partitions, like one would see at an amusement park, stated, "Visiting hours begin at 10am" and led to an area designated the Spirituality Visitor Center. Behind the dimly lit counter was a wide range of books and pamphlets the titles of which Julia couldn't make out from where she stood. Over to her left, past her father, who stood in the center of the large circular space surrounded by objects encased in glass as though it was a museum, was another visitor station, this one called the Science Visitor Center. As at the Spirituality Visitor Center, darkened lighting behind the science counter hid the names of books and pamphlets on its shelves.

Julia weaved through the maze of line partitions that guided visitor traffic. Three bars between each partition prevented anyone from dipping under. Squeaking from the soles of her shoes from the dampness of the rain convinced her taking the long route was better than attempting to jump over and risk slipping and using either her face or neck as a crutch. She made it to the front and, before walking up to her father, she caught a quick glance at some books behind the counter. A Holy Bible was on sale next to a Quran with a book on Buddhism right next to it. Underneath were other books on meditation like *The Art of Happiness* and *The Undefeated Mind*, among many others.

"What is this place?" Julia asked Quincy as she approached him in the center of the atrium. Ignoring a car bumper encased in glass with two hands imprinted on it as if someone had stopped a moving vehicle, Julia concentrated on gold symbols carved into the marble floor. She felt like an archeologist attempting to decipher hieroglyphs in a newly discovered pyramid, except the language inscribed on the floor was not completely unfamiliar. It was math, equations of some sort. Each line was filled with foreign figures like squares, backward *E*'s, cursive *p*'s, capital *P*'s, and arrows that pointed one direction or both. The familiar notations were parentheses and *x*'s sprinkled in the equations. Julia walked around the room and counted thirteen individual equations chiseled into the floor in a rising sun pattern, each with rows of items on display behind them.

Quincy stood in silence as he watched his daughter being consumed by her own curiosity. It made him think back on all the times he had received orders away from home, when he had missed opportunities to see her eyes widen at new information. Marie had had to relay all of Julia's important firsts to him by mail or phone—first ride on a bike without training wheels, first sight of a shooting star, first date, first breakup. His wife was long deceased now and all that was left behind was the child created through their union. Julia was not a kid anymore and he had no way to go back in time. Quincy vowed to be present in Julia's adult life for the new experiences soon to shatter her perceptions.

"This, baby girl, is where the periodic table meets the Gospels, where a guru can read up on alchemy. This is spirituality rooted in science or vice versa, depending on your beliefs." Quincy stretched his arms out wide, attempting to display all the wonders in the room at once. He placed his arms back to his side with a shrug as he noticed Julia taking her time staring at the floor. "It's a government agency dedicated to finding the truth of all things, the Axiom Research Agency."

Julia figured; an accepted truth is hard to find in 2022. The right slanders the left based on their version of the truth, while the left defames the right based on its own virtues. All podcasts have their own flavor of barbershop talk, a host or panel of guests spewing out opinions on *how to write* or a *new album that may be a flop.* Even the more intellectual podcast hosts use one batch of research data that bests suits the argument of the day while another pulls from a distinct set just to say *it's not true!* Julia couldn't fathom how anyone here could come to an agreement between the Big Bang or a Loud, Booming Voice.

"You're looking at Kurt Gödel's ontological proof," Quincy said, walking over to Julia, who was kneeling for a better look at the gold letters inscribed on the floor.

"Ontologi—."

"Axioms that explain God," Quincy explained as he knelt beside his daughter.

"Like y'all's Ten Commandments?"

Quincy let out a laugh that echoed throughout the room, causing some employees walking to their offices to stare in disgust. "Not even close. Say that any louder and the science guys will have a meltdown. These are more like our mission statement. There's thirteen separate lines that are axioms, definitions, or theorems."

The Ax.1, Ax.2, Df.1, or Th.4 that preceded each line now made a little more sense to Julia. "What makes Kurt Gödel so special they based a government agency on his work?"

"Well, he's mostly known as the mathematician who developed the Incompleteness Theorem. Some people in his own field hated him because he proved we as humans don't know shit about numbers, or at least all there is to know. In his old age, he came up with proof that we don't know shit about life either. He used logic symbols in his axioms to explain that, if an object has a positive property like love, for example, then it received that trait from a source. And if a source with godlike properties exists, then it must be essential for all objects. Gödel even states that necessary existence is a positive property. He broke God down into a bunch of if-and-then statements like in coding, similar to the Bible and other spiritual texts. If you do this, then you'll have a better life, or if you do this, then you'll die. It's quite fascinating."

Julia stood. "Why haven't I heard of this agency before?"

Quincy rose as well, but with a puzzled look on his face as if it were he who was processing new information. "Well, the rest of the world isn't ready to accept what most citizens of Cardinal-Wood have grown accustomed to. Not everyone can fathom spirituality and science coexisting. Plus the government shadow-bans every mention or picture of this place posted on the Internet. I mean, look around you."

Julia's attention turned toward the rows of items on display, each separately encased under glass on a miniature square column: a grape the size of a watermelon with no sign of rotting; a fang the size of Julia's hand next to a picture of a house cat that could pass as a black panther on the lap of its smiling owner, both cozily posing on an orange couch. One way Julia could tell the difference was the sharpness of the snout versus the rounded faces of the predators in the jungle. The description on the display column made it clear. "Once sweet and small. Rest in Peace, Mr. Chess. You died for science! – Jake Plume." Julia walked back over to the car bumper with the handprint indented into its steel. The placard for this display said only a name, "Roberto Almienz."

"This guy was a street racer in the nineties who stopped a car with his bare hands only to be killed by a gun. He thought he was invincible. Turns out he only had super strength," Quincy said, walking over. "This is one of the few areas besides our observatory open to the public. We call it the Axiom Museum. I can't take you to the basement; you need a special visitor's badge from the center for that, but I can show you my office."

"There's a basement?" Julia followed her father down a corridor he used his badge to open.

"There's always a basement and things the eye can't see."

They walked down the bright corridor with lights reflecting off the marble floors, past many rooms, each with its own keypad to control entrance. Quincy stopped toward the end of the hallway where only three doors remained, an emergency exit and doors to two offices across from each other. He held his badge up toward the door parading a black placard and gold lettering stating, "Asst. Director Thurman." Quincy swung the door open after a click from the lock and led Julia inside.

Julia's amazement at her father's position almost kept her silent. Words were lodged out of order in her throat. Eyes wide with wonder, she took in all the office offered. Quincy dropped his bag behind a large oak desk with a parking lot view and took a seat. A bonsai tree positioned next to his laptop partially hid his face until he leaned back in his chair. Two ceiling-high bookcases stacked with books on both sides of the room provided the main decor.

"Dad, how'd you get this job if the place technically doesn't exist?" Julia said, finally forming the sentence trapped in her vocal cords. She sat down in a chair facing her father's desk.

"The board reached out to me before my retirement last year. The assistant director of the spiritual wing was retiring himself, so the higher-ups figured a chaplain from the U.S. Navy who doubled as a Cardinal-Wood native would be a perfect fit."

"Nothing about this place makes sense." Julia leaned forward with her hands interlocked.

"That's why it's needed in a town like Cardinal-Wood. The A.R.A. employs theologians from every religion and scientists from every field. Physicists and biologists can meet with a professor of Islamic theology and a Christian assistant director to discuss the unexplainable. Field agents from both sides investigate these phenomena. I've performed exorcisms removing demons of wrath and depression from individuals while some across the building believe therapy is the way to go. Who says they're wrong? And who can say I haven't seen long-lasting peace return to a person after one of my sessions? We as a civilization have tapped into radio waves, microwaves, Wi-Fi, and Bluetooth technology. We can see bacteria hidden to the naked eye and the stars above because of magnified lenses. What else is invisible to us behind our flawed perceptions and one-sided arguments? The nosebleeds outsiders experience are just the tip of the iceberg. I believe there's something in the air. Everything okay, baby girl?"

The sound of tapping on glass had resumed somewhere between Julia's gut and her heart. It snapped and creaked its way up to her ears, past her own skepticism about an invisible God preached by a once-absent father. The image of the Libby–Marie hybrid flashed once more in her mind before shattering again.

Julia had found it difficult to believe in the ethereal as a child while the physical things she desired were absent or drunk. Two words her father said echoed in Julia's short-term memory. *Flawed perceptions.* What else had she missed by looking through the lens of a child or of pure ignorance? What else had she missed because of not viewing the situation at the right *frequency*? With that thought came an image of Zander and his electric smile, causing her stomach to turn. Maybe it was the McGriddles, but Julia had a feeling her nightmare was something more than a bad dream and she needed to check on him immediately.

"Yeah, Dad, I'm fine. I just remembered I have to take care of a few things before work. See you later tonight, okay?" Julia shook her head as she stood.

"Alright, baby girl, thanks for the ride," Quincy said, but Julia didn't hear. She was already out the door.

If good exists, then evil does too.

That's an axiom Julia wanted to add to the list of the A.R.A's ontological equations. Dwelling on Libby's razor-toothed snarl mixed with her mother's face had Julia's heart in a vice grip, thumping to break free. She tried calling Zander, but his phone went straight to voicemail, increasing her fear. It was a quarter past eleven now and Julia was out of possible explanations for why Zander wasn't answering. She also couldn't tell if her nightmare was simply that or an elaborate warning.

The downpour continued in Cardinal-Wood as Julia drove north toward Zander's apartment. Exploring the five districts of C-W wasn't in her morning plans but her GPS said traffic on 95-N would take forty-five minutes to go from Braenfries to Amada Grove. Taking the main roads cutting through Lyn City would take only thirty minutes. During her brief stay in this large county, Julia hadn't yet found her bearings on the ins and outs of each district. Tall buildings were everywhere and she had just learned about a secret government agency in the suburbs. She knew, though, that Lyn City was the official downtown of the county. It boasted the most shops, stores, and restaurants per block, including The Pit.

A right here, a left four miles down the road, and she was in a familiar part of Lyn City, determined to drive past her place of employment. Zander's apartment was just five minutes up the road but flashing blue and red lights in front of The Pit forced her to slow down. She almost caused an accident while doing so. The driver behind her blared his horn and yelled a slur before pulling around and kicking up rainwater as he sped away. Julia was too deep inside her head to hear anything.

*Oh, God, no.* Julia counted four cop cars parked parallel to the building's entrance. Their lights danced off the puddles surrounding the brick structure. Funny how the mind cries out for external help when there are no answers within. This did not humor Julia. It only filled her with dread as she parked her car, her heart breaking free of its restraints and sinking into her stomach with each step toward The Pit.

# 3

## SORRY I MISSED YOUR CALL

*Hey, this is Zander Thurman. Sorry I missed your call. If this is a business inquiry—*. Julia ended the call before the voicemail message could finish. Sheltered from the storm by the red canopy hanging over The Pit's entrance, she hoped her despair would pass at the sound of Zander's voice but the recording only strengthened it.

*Maybe I should've gone to his house first thing this morning.* Julia remembered a childhood nightmare of her mom dying in a car crash. She had rushed to her mother's room in the middle of the night and held her finger to Marie's nose for proof she was alive and well. She also recalled making Marie go through hell and actual high water to get in touch with Quincy, who was deployed out at sea, because of a *feeling.* Quincy had laughed and asked if his daughter was speaking to the universe because he was experiencing a bad case of food poisoning from crab legs served on the ship but everything else was okay.

If Julia had stepped out of her own head for one moment and checked on Zander with the urgency of her childhood, this guilt cocktail wouldn't be churning in her stomach. One thing about adulting: personal problems always seem more difficult than those of others until reality makes an objection. Julia watched as the wind blew rain onto The Pit's welcome sign and decided to go inside. She went from one storm to the next.

Inside, down the hall dressed in red carpet, a man in a brown trench coat stood with his back turned at the podium. The coat, stained by raindrops, swallowed the frail-framed man, who was admiring the fabric of the curtain separating the waiting and dining areas. His sharp nose pointed upward with no attention to the opening or closing of the front door as his narrow wrist reached for the rope to close the curtain between the rooms. Julia took five steps before freezing.

The scent of lavender locked her brain and knees in place. Next the taste of honey rushed over her tongue and took her thoughts to a place where doubt, grief, and anxiety failed to exist. A face Julia had met the day before focused in her mind's eye. *Libby Yolke.* Libby's smooth skin was illuminated by a sun-colored aura. The black locks flowing past Libby's shoulders intensified the lavender scent creeping up Julia's nose as they swayed from side to side. Libby led Julia away from her concern for Zander to a cliff where water crashed against the rocks below.

"Jump and I'll take care of the rest," Libby said, seduction softening her voice.

Julia inched toward the edge, glancing down at the battle raging between the rocks and the water. One more step and she could let everything go. Maybe she would find joy at the bottom. Or would she find fleeting happiness? Peace could be her reward. Or would her reward be pandemonium that greeted her on the tip of the rocks?

The sound of cracking glass inside Julia's heart accompanied these questions, growing louder each moment as it rose from her chest to her ears. It silenced the rushing waves beneath. She took a step back and the image projected in her thoughts shattered. While the impression fell Julia caught a glimpse of Libby, whose smile quickly turned into that snarl exposing razor-sharp teeth. Then everything faded to black.

"Excuse me, miss, is everything okay? Hello?"

The fog covering Julia's eyes slowly dissipated. The man in the trench coat turned to face Julia while his body pointed toward the curtain and his hand still held the golden rope. Julia looked back at the entrance as her vision cleared. She counted the number of steps she had taken forward from the front door without control of her own limbs; it was roughly ten paces.

Julia could no longer ignore the snapping sound that rang deep in her gut and up to her ears, the sensation of shattering perceived realities she had experienced twice already. The first had awakened her from her nightmare the night before. The second came after her father's tour of the A.R.A. It vibrated louder than any stomach growl she had heard her body make before and no doubt broke her free from that illusion. Her face tightened with assurance but loosened as doubt set in. Had she experienced a nightmare at all, or a failed hijacking?

"Ah, ma'am, if you're not in an emergency, one of the employees will be right with you to help," the man said, struggling to master the curtain's pulley system.

"I'm looking for—." Julia hadn't finished her statement before Bianca burst through the curtain.

"Excuse me! I told you I'd close the curtain after seating my guests," Bianca scolded the man, paying no attention to Julia. Bianca's eyes widened enough to force both of his hands off the rope and into the air.

*What's she doing here?* Bianca should have been snacking on peanuts, flying toward Egypt by now.

"I apologize. I didn't want our lights disturbing the patrons of this lovely place you have here," the man, a cop, said, putting his hands down. "You have a new visitor, by the way."

Bianca shifted her focus to Julia, pausing for a moment afterward. Julia noticed small flickers in Bianca's eyes as though two candles were positioned in the windowsills of her soul. The dim lights in Bianca's pupils went out as she spoke. "Oh, no, Julia. You shouldn't be here. Why aren't you with your family?" Bianca walked up to Julia and wrapped her in a comforting hug.

"What are you doing here?" Julia meant to ask Bianca, but "What's going on?" came out instead. She was not able to ignore the inevitable any longer. "I've been trying to reach Zander all morning and stopped here on my way to his apartment."

"What's your name, miss?" the officer asked, stepping forward. His eyes sharpened to match the edges of his cheekbones.

"This was—is—Zander Thurman's cousin Julia. She started working here yesterday," Bianca said, taking the liberty to deliver the introduction. Her hand floated behind Julia's back, patting it softly.

The man closed his eyes and grimaced as if his bare foot had stepped on a patch of Legos. After adjusting the loosely fitted coat properly over his shoulders, he composed himself and said, "Detective Stubbs, ma'am." He flashed a badge on the inside of his coat. "I hate to inform you that your cousin Zander Thurman has passed."

The weight of confirmation collapsed over Julia's soul, condemning her conscience to a series of shame-filled reprimands. *I should've gone this morning. Dream or not, I should've gone.* Her heart thumped fast enough that the beat clogged her ears as her legs trembled, ready to give way.

"What happened?" Julia asked, with a quiver breaking through. Bianca tightened her grasp around Julia's shoulders. A whiff of lavender grazed Julia's nostrils, placing a dam over the exits from where emotions spill. The ongoing guilt-ridden mental assault inside of Julia slowly chipped away at the invisible walls.

"We received a call around 7:15 this morning about a smell coming from his apartment. Found him face down on his keyboard. He had a dry-erase board hanging on the wall with his schedule on it, so my partner and I figured we would come down here while the forensics guys handled the scene, to see if anything was *off* when he was last here."

Julia shrugged off Bianca's arm and sat on a bench in the waiting area. The comfort from an acquaintance had reached its limit. She trusted the inanimate object to help her bear the weight of this bad news. She folded her hands over her head as she tried to make sense of it all. The image of Libby reappeared in her head, whispering to Julia that *everything was okay.* Julia suppressed her tears and focused on the ambition and generosity of her electric cousin, the laughter between them during family trips in the past, how he had helped her get a new job in a strange town. Zander had never allowed himself to be sidetracked from his vision of delivering entertainment. He always aimed forward. Remembering the true essence of his character crumbled the Libby-constructed dam in Julia's soul and the tears began to pour out.

Julia's hands, pressed hard to her face, cupped the water spilling from her eyes. The tears rolled down her face without a whimper or a wail. Her sadness was short-lived as she redirected the tears of grief into tears of rage. Someone was responsible for all of this, for everything from Zander's death to Julia's own mental and body manipulations. The police had to talk to Libby Yolke.

"He left with some actress for his next skit. Her name was Libby Yolke," Julia said while drying her face and hands with the sleeve of her shirt.

Neither Julia or Detective Stubbs noticed Bianca's eyes widen before quickly regaining their sympathetic glow.

"Hold that thought, please. I need you to repeat that for my partner," Stubbs said. "Bianca, could you lead us back to your office?"

"Sure, follow me." Bianca scampered through the curtain opening.

Julia trailed Detective Stubbs while Bianca led the way around the dining area. They walked through the kitchen, passing cooks, busboys, waiters, and waitresses hiding from their tables, before stopping at a back room with Bianca's name engraved on the door. Bianca Munier. One of the perks to being both owner and manager is your name carrying more weight than either title ever could.

Bianca moved aside, allowing Stubbs to approach the door.

"Bullaby, we're coming in," Stubbs said before swinging the door open.

Kyle sat with his back toward the entrance, facing Bianca's desk, as a giant in a black trench coat towered over his right side, scribbling in an open notepad.

"I got the cousin of the deceased here. She actually gave us the name of who he left with last night," Detective Stubbs said, guiding Julia inside.

The detective finished jotting down his thoughts with a click of his pen, which looked more like a needle in his enormous hand. He glanced up from his notes, displaying a face salted by experience. Steady eyes unshaken from the news delivered by his partner countered the grinding teeth under his grey-peppered beard.

"Detective Bullaby," he said, flashing his CWPD badge on the inside of his coat. "Please take a seat against the wall and I'll be right with you." He directed Julia with his pen.

"I'm gonna go back to the front," Bianca said from the doorway as Julia picked a chair lined against the wall and sat down.

"I'll head up there with you. Let me know if you need anything, Bullaby," Detective Stubbs said before dragging the office door shut.

Kyle turned toward Julia, revealing a dim reflective glow in his eyes. It was the same glow a deer's eyes reflect from an oncoming car's headlights before becoming acquainted with the car's grill. Kyle, though, didn't have the same dumbfounded look the beasts of the woods wear when greeted with death. His nose flared up, tugging his lip into a snarl, and he turned back to face Detective Bullaby.

Staring at the closed door, Bullaby shook his head, then clicked his pen and continued taking notes.

"Mr. Mitchell, continue telling me about this woman who left with your friend yesterday." Bullaby directed his glare downward at Kyle.

"Well, like I said earlier, she was the most beautiful human I've ever laid eyes on. Short, brown hair, brown eyes, round lips. Five two at most. A tattoo of a snake coming from her shoulder to her earlobe as if it was trying to eat the whole thing."

"So you remember all this but don't remember her name?" Bullaby did not bother to hide his skepticism.

"I mean, I wish I could, but there's a blank spot in my head whenever I try to remember it. Almost like the name is hiding from me." Kyle rubbed his hands over his temples, attempting to massage the information out.

"That's a lie. I don't know why he's lying to you, but that's not what she looked like." Julia paused, searching past potholes of raged and grief in her mind in order to collect the right words to end this charade.

"Your cousin is dead and you think I have time to play games? You're a fucking trip." Kyle turned back to Julia. Sockets swollen by tears had extinguished and replaced the dim lights that flickered in his eyes.

"Shut up or we'll continue this talk at the precinct," Bullaby said. Julia swore a paper weight on Bianca's desk vibrated at Bullaby's slightly raised voice.

Kyle turned back around and put his head down in silence. "Please continue," Bullaby said to Julia.

"She was at least five foot five, just under my line of sight. Her eyes were more like two amber fires than brown. Black locks from her head to her shoulders. A small frame, blessed in all the right areas. And I don't remember seeing any tattoos on her."

"Uh-huh. Thought you had a name with this description."

"Libby Yolke."

"Okay." Bullaby finished jotting down this new information in his notepad. He took his cell phone out once he finished and, after two taps on the screen, held it to his ear. "Stubbs, bring the manager back to the office. I have a couple questions for her."

A few silent moments passed that were interrupted by a knock at the door. Stubbs allowed Bianca to walk in first, then closed the door behind them. Bianca stood next to Julia instead of taking a seat while Stubbs remained with his back to the door.

"Ms. Munier, you described the person who left with Zander as a tall woman, at least five foot ten, correct?" Bullaby asked, flipping back through pages in his notebook.

"That's correct."

"Black hair stopping at her shoulders with her ends dyed blue. And, I quote, *'the smoothest skin I've ever seen. She could have been a life-sized Barbie doll.'*" Bullaby ended the quote in a slow lull.

"What the fu—?" Kyle cut himself off once he locked eyes with Bullaby, whose teeth were again noticeably grinding underneath his shifting beard.

"Do you need me to write it down for you?" Bianca hissed. "I don't understand the confusion."

"Please calm down. All three of you have given different descriptions of who's supposed to be the same person. And only one of you could give a name. So ya'll are either fucking with me or fucking yourselves over in the long run. Could anyone else describe this woman to us?" Bullaby asked.

"Bobby saw her, Bobby Velle, but he's not in today," Bianca said. "I could pull up the security footage from yesterday. I can access the system through my computer." She pointed to her desk.

"If you're giving us consent, then go right ahead," Bullaby said, moving aside so Bianca could take a seat behind the monitor.

After a few clicks of the mouse, Julia couldn't hold her tongue through the silence of the loading screen. "What happened to your trip, Bianca?"

Bianca lifted her head from the glowing display. Her eyes held a shimmering light projected from somewhere deeper than the computer she was facing.

Bullaby answered for Bianca. "Excuse me. We're the ones with the badges." He pointed at himself and Stubbs. "We're the ones who get to ask the questions."

"It's okay, Detective. It's hard to lose a loved one. Questioning everything around you in a situation like that is normal," Bianca said to Bullaby before directing her attention back to Julia with a fading light trapped in her eyes. "They called me right as I was boarding my flight and told me the news. Said they needed help retracing Zander's steps after finding his schedule." She sighed, letting an air of sympathy creep into her voice. "There's no way I would've been able to enjoy Egypt knowing what had happened. Zander was like family to me."

Sometimes it is easier to accept a lie because digging for the truth requires work. At other times, it is best to let a lie cultivate while you gather tools to exterminate it. Julia kept quiet, clenching her fists in her lap to the point her fingers went numb.

"Here we are." Bianca rolled away from the screen so Bullaby could look. The sparkle in her eye faded as she and Bullaby watched the security footage play.

Unable to see the monitor for themselves, Julia and Kyle could only watch the faces of the two viewers. Bullaby's tightened jaw dragged his eyebrows down. Bianca's eyes, absent their ethereal electricity, went from sympathetic to wide with shock. One could imagine that was how Bianca had looked when she had received the call from the cops, but Julia, after many years of training in skepticism, found that hard to believe.

Bullaby scratched his beard and turned the screen around with his free hand. "You two able to explain this to me?"

It took a few moments for Julia's brain to register what she was seeing. The same could be said for Kyle, who sat staring with his mouth wide open. All he could do was let tears build up in his eyes. Even Stubbs leaned in for a better angle.

The footage from the day before revealed Julia, Kyle, and Bianca standing by the podium minutes before Zander returned with Bobby. Julia's head shook back and forth once she recognized the moment Bianca had attempted to laugh off Kyle's joke about extending her trip. Immediately the attention of the three on the screen turned toward the entrance. Entranced by an unseen force, Julia, Kyle, and Bianca froze in place, almost as if they were practicing for CWPD booking photos. A few words were mumbled between them in the midst of their immobility. Tears gathered in Julia's eyes as well, threatening to erode the last bit of sanity in her soul.

Zander made his debut, strolling into the security footage with Bobby trailing right behind. Bobby wobbled along until his feet locked in the next available spot of the makeshift viewing gallery while Zander continued forward. After taking a couple steps toward the exit, Zander turned back to the group. Not completely mesmerized, Bobby tried forming words until stopped by a wave from Zander's hand.

Bullaby paused the tape. What was hidden from Julia a day before revealed itself with blinding illumination. Zander's eyes held a bright, glowing light that accompanied his presidential smile and executive wave confined in the image of the still frame. The light was too vibrant for Julia to consider it a simple glare from the camera's lens, especially after what she'd witnessed from Kyle and Bianca. For a moment she thought the light danced and pulsated through the paused screen but she found out it was only the water built up in her own eyes tumbling down her face. At least that's what a piece of her *wanted to believe*.

"I swear he left with someone!" Julia said, struggling to keep her voice steady.

"This ain't right. It's all—it's all fucked up and it ain't right. There has to be something wrong with the recording." Kyle had less control over his trembling voice.

"Well, our cyber forensics team will be able to validate the tape, but you're right. This is fucked up, starting with you three. I could charge all of you with conspiracy, bring you in, and call it a day. All I see here is a kid who is alone and happy to leave work." Bullaby turned the screen back toward Bianca. "Taking y'all to the precinct won't make this case any easier, though. If the timestamp on this video is correct and Zander was here yesterday, then there's a disconnect with the time of death given by the on-site examiner."

"What do you mean, a disconnect?" Julia asked.

Bullaby started to speak but hesitated, possibly contemplating if the news would help or damage the ears it fell on. "The body we found this morning looked like he's been deceased for a week. Maybe a couple days more."

"I have to see him." Julia stood up from her seat with her eyes leaking tears that disregarded all reason and logic.

"You don't want to see your cousin now. Just remember what he was to you. I've seen a lot of bodies in my career and none of them looked so dehydrated after one day—not even from decomposing, but absent of all water as if the life was just sucked right out of him." Bullaby signaled Stubbs with a two-fingered wave toward the door as if he was saying it was *time to go*. "Now, if any of you try to skip town and make this investigation easier for us, that would be great. If not, we'll be in touch."

Julia picked Quincy up from work so he could be by his brother's side as he and his wife claimed Zander's body. Uncle Zach, who could pass as Quincy's twin if it weren't for his bald head, fell into the wide arms shared by the Thurman men. Quincy embraced his younger brother, wrapping him in a straitjacket made of muscles in an attempt to contain Zach's hysterical wails. *"My baby boy! My god, what happened to my son?"*

Andrea, Julia's aunt, leaned on her husband's shoulder, soiling her auburn hair with cries filled with snot and tears of her own, staining Zach's green-collared shirt, yearning for an invitation to join the warm comfort of her brother-in-law's arms as well.

Julia stood in the doorway of the chilled, white-tiled room of the morgue, watching as the family gathered around Zander's corpse. With her tear reserves exhausted from the past hour, she believed she had no more to give but wondered how she would react if she stepped forward, if she was ready to confirm Bullaby's words: *"as if the life was just sucked right out of him."*

Based on her uncle's pleas, she figured Zander's body wasn't just cold and lifeless but possibly also mutilated. To see Zander for herself would validate Bullaby's observation as well as strengthen her doubts about how Zander got here. Was she ready to acknowledge she was able to see what others couldn't perceive? Was she ready to believe Zander left the building with a witch, a ghost, or something worse? Standing still made it easy to dwell on the name Libby Yolke in the realm of logic and reason. It was easier to believe the security footage was doctored than to admit to being deceived by someone or something sinister.

*But those eyes.* Julia pictured the sparks of light in Bianca and Kyle's pupils. Even Zander's eyes held that same glow within the paused frame of the footage, taking after the galaxy of stars she remembered glaring at her when she came face to face with Libby in her dream. Her blindness of yesterday was by design. Any blindness of today would be by choice. So she took a step forward.

Julia walked around her huddling family and stopped at Zander's side. A blackened husk rested in a stiff, twisted manner on the metal bed in front of her. Zander's skin looked burnt, crusty patches spread all over, dried and flaky as if he were covered in scales. He showed signs of rapid malnutrition, causing his flesh to shrink down to his bones. The pieces of his hair that remained had turned grey like stress itself was his murderer. Bullaby was right. Nothing about Zander's body was normal based on when he was last seen. All the cadavers she had studied in school confirmed that observation, from burn victims to drownings, maulings, and overdoses, to straight-up murders. None of that prepared Julia to see one of her family members on a slab.

The pleasant scent of lavender made its way up to Julia's nose from Zander's corpse. Surprised to not be greeted by the smell of decay, Julia widened her eyes and took a step back.

*Julia*

*Julia*

*Julia*

A soft voice lodged in her head cried out.

"*Juliaaa,*" Zander's corpse whispered, stretching out a frail, decrepit hand.

The family members locked in Quincy's bear hug didn't hear a word. Only Julia had been spellbound by the calling of her name.

"*Juliaaaa, don't you see?*" Zander's corpse asked as the fragile bones in his arm cracked as he stretched it forward. He slowly pulled Julia closer, closer, and closer until she saw what the dead wanted her to see.

The room around Julia went black. Like a switch of a TV channel, the lights of another room cut on. Julia had been far removed from the cold walls of the morgue and placed behind the computer of someone's home office. The surrounding space blurred as if she was looking through the eyes of person in their late seventies slowly going blind. Movie posters hung on the walls: *Pulp Fiction,* *Clerks,* and Christopher Nolan's *Dark Knight Rises.* None of these gave Julia a clue to where she had been transported until she noticed the dry-erase board hanging next to the door.

"This Week's Schedule" was written in bright, bold, red letters: "7pm filming, 9pm editing, 6am drafting" were highlighted throughout the week in purple, blue, and orange dry-erase markers. Another entry scattered around the board titled "Pit hours" was highlighted in green with the latest entry for Sunday, just the day before. Julia turned back toward the computer as the monitor switched to a generic black screen saver, reflecting a face that wasn't her own.

Julia looked through Zander's dull yet alive eyes as he reached for the keyboard. Her hands were his hands or his hands were hers. In this moment she acted as an avatar robbed of active participation, becoming a distant observer.

The computer's display lit up. Zander scrolled up toward the top of a document. Bypassing four pages, he stopped at a title—*Excuse me, I ordered the sandwich, not the wrap: The Eden Gardens Royale.*

"I think we can call it a night." Zander clicked the save button.

A soft word responded from behind him. "You sure? It's only two in the morning. Why don't we do an all-nighter just to say we did?" Each word massaged the ridges in Zander's brain. Julia, aware of the voice that chimed like a tuning fork in her ears as well as Zander's, felt her heart beating through her chest upon remembering where she last heard that tune.

Zander turned from his computer to a beautiful woman with blonde hair sitting on a blue futon against the wall. Her cheekbones were sharp, outlined by the hair hanging to her shoulders. Her green eyes shone bright like traffic lights, encouraging the two cousins to go forward.

There was something familiar about her beauty to Julia. It transcended anything you could find with just a scroll through social media. The sensation of Julia's heart beating as if it were trying to break out of her chest cavity was something she had experienced when she saw Libby for the first time. Now, looking at this woman from Zander's perspective as he wiped the sweat gathered on his forehead, confirmed her fear.

"Come on, Libby, this script is perfect now." Zander pointed back to the computer. "Don't tempt me with a good time. I'd push on and get two more drafts done before sunrise if I didn't have to work tomorrow."

"You mean today," Libby said, a copy of the script in her hand.

"Ha, ha. You know what I meant."

*How does she look so completely different? No black locks or brown eyes. Who is she? What is she?* Julia thought as Libby rose from her seat.

Libby's green eyes began to pulsate, snapping Julia's unanswered questions into many pieces like dry fall leaves crumbling under a hiker's boot.

"I guess you're right, Zander. I believe we've had enough fun for the night," Libby said as she leaned over Zander's shoulder and placed her copy of the script on his desk. She inched back but remained close to Zander's face. They locked onto each other's eyes as Libby's continued to emit an enticing emerald glow. "You're burning up," she said, resting the back of her hand on Zander's forehead.

Captivated by the flashing light, Zander failed to respond. His jaw dropped as his breathing intensified, leaving room for air to only pass through in this dumbfounded state. From within, Julia became ensnared by the shine of Libby's eyes as well. Her mind drifted toward nothingness as Zander's vision blurred the corners of the room, leaving the focus on Libby, whose face advertised a hungry grin.

"I think I may have burnt you out sooner than expected." Libby removed her hand from Zander's forehead. She ironed out the hunch in her back and stood tall. "*Viral, viral, viral.* That word rang so loud in your head, I couldn't stop you, even if I wanted to, from throwing yourself over the ledge right into the depths of the digital plague engulfing this generation." She continued, towering over Zander like a cat playing with its next meal. Her smile grew wider, exposing teeth that sharpened into knifelike edges. Her voice transitioned from a soothing tone to rough and mangled, as if a wood chipper was spitting out each word. "It's always the same with you humans, no matter the time. Fame and fortune. Beauty and knowledge. This era is my favorite by far. With all of you busy looking at each other, there's no time to build a foundation for yourselves. I hear millions of cries in the night calling my name, trading their lives for a season of pleasure."

Libby stretched out her hand and the image of a human arm melted away. Pieces of skin fell, dissipating before they reached the floor. She placed a grey hand on Zander's cheek covered with cracks that looked like scales. Black talons replaced her manicured nails pressed against Zander's flesh.

Julia felt Zander's chest tighten as if a cinder block was strapped to it, speeding up his descent into the depths of despair. Tears flowed from his eyes as he faced the unimaginable. Zander mumbled a phrase garbled by his own air, just as someone who is about to drown makes their last cry. "Wh-what's going on, Libby? Why?"

"Unchecked ambition isn't good for the soul. Blame this on yourself, Zander, and the thorns you gathered on your road to glory."

What happened next terrified Julia so much she thought her heart exploded. Maybe it did, because she stopped breathing for a few moments after and it felt like her eyes were ready to pop out of their sockets.

Similar to her dream, the smooth skin hiding Libby's true face dissolved into the air, revealing what Julia could only describe to herself as a *monster*. Dry, cracking, grey scales covered the creature's head from scalp to chin. Its jawline with teeth of knives stretched into an ear-to-ear grin, mimicking the demeanor of a great white shark. Darkness consumed the eyes' pulsating green light until the twirl of a shrinking galaxy shone brightly inside. The mirage of the blonde hair faded away, replaced by a floating crown of seven golden spikes vertically lined across its skull. Libby's clothes transformed into a black robe as she looked down on Zander like a judge passing a sentence of damnation.

"You have fallen into the natural order of things. Now I must feed." The creature known as Libby Yolke gripped Zander's temples. Its mouth opened wide with a shriek, exposing several rows of dagger-like teeth hiding behind the large razors of the front row and clamped down on Zander's skull.

Julia didn't hear the sound of cracked bones as the monster's teeth tightened. Piercing a place deeper than the skeleton, a sloshing noise rang between Zander's ears like his brain was being blended into a smoothie, sending both his body and Julia's soul into shock. Zander was in a comatose state, unable to scream as his hands and feet twitched violently. Drool spilled from his lips while Libby drained him of nutrients like a leech.

Stuck between two moments in time—past and present—as well as two places—the morgue's floor and Zander's body—Julia felt her soul being carried away too. Her heart thumped against the cold tiles as her body convulsed on the ground. In the thickening darkness covering her mind, Julia saw the monstrous Libby pull away from Zander with a sigh as if it had just finished a refreshing drink.

Zander's eyes rolled back and forth in his head, catching glimpses of the star-filled pupils looking back at him, "You taste special today," Libby hissed, pausing before sinking her teeth in for another gulp. Zander went limp in the jaws of the monster as his life force evaporated from his body.

It was the end, at least as Julia was concerned, of the scented memory passed on to her by Zander's corpse. She gave up holding onto consciousness, strained by the experience. Pleas from her father reached her ears before she completely passed out.

"Julia, wake up! Wake up, baby girl! Oh, God, please," Quincy cried out.

The prayer never made it to her ears but hopefully God heard it Julia thought as her presence in the present drifted away.

A beeping tone synched with Julia's heartbeat startled her awake. Her body felt heavy, as if an avalanche had crushed her under layers of snow. The sense of delirium that attaches itself to most wake-up routines cleared as Julia pieced together her surroundings. Sunlight ricocheted off the tiled floor while she lay tucked in a hospital bed. Quincy sat in a chair next to her, sleeping with his arms folded.

Julia dragged her IV-pierced hand to her forehead, rattling the equipment. Her head throbbed as the memory of how she got here reloaded into her brain. She wished to forget what she saw. Trying to rationalize how she could see it even made her stomach do backflips. The scented memory of Zander's death was imprinted on her mind the same way the *fear of the dark* is imprinted on the consciousness of all humankind. She wanted to deny the proof that her dream was something more, that an otherworldly predator was on the loose. It only reminded her how late she was, how she couldn't save Zander. Before grief and guilt made her finish her wish to share Zander's fate instead of confronting the truth, Quincy woke up.

"Hey, baby girl, I'm here. How you feeling?" Quincy said, leaning out of his seat to lightly hug his daughter in a way she was too weak to reciprocate.

"I'm okay, Dad, but—." Julia felt something simmering on the inside, something rampaging deeper than her stomach, closer to her soul. "Zander was murdered. I saw it for myself," Julia whimpered as she wrapped her weak arm around his shoulder.

"What do you mean, you saw it?" Quincy asked, pulling away with scrunched eyebrows that shifted his glasses.

"I don't know how. Maybe it was a vision or some sort of mental email, but Zander left with who I thought was a woman yesterday. I saw she was in his apartment last night working with him on his scripts until she—." Julia paused as the pings from the heart monitor grew more frequent. Her drained body couldn't keep up with her excitement. "The woman transformed into a monster." Another word for Libby sprouted from Julia's lips. "No, she was a demon, not simply a creature that hides under the bed. She was something sinister. Her eyes, her teeth. Oh, God, those teeth—."

Quincy remained silent as his eyebrows continued to mold confusion onto his face. He opened his mouth to speak but couldn't find the words. He remembered a time long before Julia was born when Marie had relayed a similar message complaining about monsters hiding around the corner or inside a kitchen cabinet, hideous creatures peeking into this world as if the earth was placed in an aquarium tank shielded by glass. He had nothing to say to his wife to relieve her hysteria. He had only a suggestion: *leave the county and never come back.* So he and the woman *of* his dreams ran. Marie followed him around the world once he joined the military, but her memories from looking behind life's spiritual curtain never left. Where Quincy couldn't provide absolute peace, Marie tried to find it in alcohol. He made her run from something she couldn't escape. Now he was back where it all had started, back home with his daughter, who was battling the same demons. Running wasn't an option this time.

"It's okay, Julia, I believe you." Quincy placed an arm on her shoulder. He could feel her breathing return to normal as her body relaxed.

"How can you believe me when I barely believe this shit?" Julia asked, trying to block off her one avenue of assurance in the middle of this madness.

"Because Cardinal-Wood forces everyone to embrace the unexplainable," Quincy said, leaving the truth about Marie Thurman as a story to tell another day.

"We have to tell the cops. Two detectives came by The Pit this morning. I can try to get ahold of them."

Quincy grimaced. "That was yesterday, baby girl. You've been out for a whole day. Plus, the police claimed Zander's death was a suicide. Said he overworked himself without eating properly. They described it as a case of malnutrition."

Terror overtook Julia's face as she placed her head in her hands. She felt like screaming but couldn't gather the energy. *This can't be happening!*

"Look, when you get on your feet, I'll get you a cleared visitor's pass to show you what we're working on in the basement at the A.R.A. We can help."

Julia had nothing else to say and Quincy had nothing else to reveal, so the two sat in silence. The next few hours were a muted blur before Julia told Quincy he could go home and get some rest. She'd call him tomorrow if she was going to be discharged from the hospital, but right now she needed to spend some time alone to process everything.

Deep into the night as moonlight illuminated her face, Julia lay wide awake in her hospital bed. The feeling of something rampaging inside of her returned, just as it had when she spoke with her father earlier. She dwelled on Zander, on her own failures, and how she couldn't even keep herself out of the hospital by using her newly discovered gift of shattering perceived realities. It had saved her during Libby's attempted nighttime hijacking of her mind and when she had walked into The Pit before she received the news about Zander, but it didn't help when she faced death. There was no reason to count on an ability she could not control—*yet*. Clouds slowly covered the moon, adding shadows to an already dark room. A sense of someone or something watching her crossed Julia's mind but the ravaging beast in her own soul overrode that inclination. She didn't care what Libby was. Julia knew *it* had to be stopped. The beast clawing at the cage inside of Julia's spirit finally broke free and its name was Resolve. It reminded her of some primal instinct ingrained in humans since the days local villagers gathered to slay the beast terrorizing the nearby forest. She was going to kill a monster.

Ϥ

# AGENT OF TRUTH

*Just have a little faith.* Julia tried nurturing the words her father recited on their way into the Axiom Research Agency. She wanted to cultivate the phrase filled with budding optimism into her own garden she could feed from when the season was right. During the car ride to the A.R.A. she asked him how anyone in this building, not related to her, would believe what she had seen and if it was even possible to fight a demonic entity from another plane of existence.

"Faith goes a long way, baby girl," Quincy said, continuing the conversation while using his badge to buzz open the front door. Julia followed suit and held her new badge to the card reader at the second door of the main entrance. A green light flashed over the card reader and she pulled the door open, looking over at the Spirituality Visitor's entrance before walking in. In the two days since Julia had been discharged from the hospital, her father had obtained high enough credentials to get Julia through the front door.

"When you said the A.R.A. could help me, I didn't think I'd get my own badge." Julia clipped the badge with her headshot onto her shirt. When Quincy texted her asking for a clear photo of her face while she was still in the hospital, she took her own selfie with matted hair and patient gown visible because the last picture she had of herself was from 2018.

"Nepotism is a gift all parents wish to extend to their kids. Also, someone higher than me took an interest in your story and made a couple calls. C'mon, we have to get going," Quincy said, speed walking through the museum's marbled floors. He paid no attention to the gold equations etched into the ground or the items enclosed in glass. It was a normal workday for him. Julia moved through the space in awe, hoping to view something new during her second visit. She followed Quincy as he rushed down the corridor leading to his office.

"I just have to drop off my bag and both of us need to leave our phones up here before we head downstairs. This man is as punctual as a nail," Quincy said, reaching his office door. He pushed his badge toward the reader to gain access.

Julia took her phone out of her pocket and looked at the black screen. Her notifications had been relatively stale since she got out of the hospital. Most messages or calls came from Quincy, all except one from Bianca this morning.

*Bianca: I know this is difficult. Take as much time as you need. Please let me know if your extended family at The Pit can do anything to help.*

A thousand-legged tingle crawled up Julia's spine like a centipede after rereading the text for the fourth time. Doubts that Bianca had typed that under her own free will came to mind because the spark in her eyes was like one out of the billions nestled in Libby's pupils. The same went for Kyle and Zander. If that light meant Libby's charm marked them, Julia figured her first step to stopping Libby would be to sever the connection she had with those around her. The message remained unanswered. Julia locked her phone as she stood next to her father in front of his office.

The metal of the door's deadbolt clanked and Quincy pushed the door open, pausing before taking a step inside. His mouth dropped to the floor as quickly as the bag in his hand did.

"If I'm the nail of punctuality, then blame my mother for hammering me into the wall," a low, raspy voice said from inside.

"Uh, good morning, Victor. I didn't expect you to be in my office. Or my chair," Quincy said, regaining his composure. Quincy collected his bag and proceeded inside.

Julia followed Quincy inside and saw a man much older than her father sitting behind his desk. Wrinkled lines branched from the corners of his eyes like many little rivers splitting and spilling into the ocean of his face. A wide smile stretched across his face, rippling those wrinkles like waves.

"Good morning, Quincy. And this must be Julia! Your father has told me a few interesting things about you," he said, extending a hand.

Julia hesitated to shake his hand while she searched his pupils for any flashing light. There were moments of tense paranoia when she felt as if Libby was stalking her, aware of Julia's escape and freedom from the mental prison she tried to trap her in, following Julia from the shadows of her father's house, hiding behind the shower curtain, or even controlling the Uber eats driver who had delivered her Chipotle last night. Unable to control her gift of heightened perception, Julia had to rely on that *little faith* Quincy spoke about and trust he knew what he was signing her up for.

"Hope none of it freaked you out," Julia said, shaking his hand.

The old man laughed with lungs degraded by cigarette smoke more so than his age. "Oh, not even close, young lady."

"Julia, this is Victor Jefferson, your new boss." Quincy placed his bag next to the desk.

"Oh. Nice to meet you, sir," Julia said, softening her face.

"How'd you get into my office, Victor? We were supposed to meet downstairs," Quincy stated, moving toward his chair.

"You're asking the man who got your daughter the proper clearance to get downstairs in less than two days how he got into *your* office? No door is closed to me. I wanted to make sure I made the right decision before you brought her down." Victor picked up a thin manila folder as he rose from the seat. "Tell me, what do you see?" he said, passing the folder to Julia.

She opened the folder and initial shock tried to pry it from her fingers. Julia saw a still shot of a man no older than Zander with red, curly hair in the middle of a live-streaming session wearing a chef's uniform. The photo captured his excitement and a few of the comments coming in as he stood over a batch of rainbow-colored pastries.

Wow, Carter, those look delicious!

How much for a dozen???

My mom's birthday is next week. U available to cater?

Julia clutched the folder tighter as she looked deeper into the searchlights beaming from Carter's pupils. She flipped to the next photo and saw a disfigured body charred and drained of all color of life. Veins protruded from his arms to his neck. His once-red hair had transitioned to a dull grey.

"H-his body. It looks like Zander's."

"Carter Smith's body was found the morning after that screenshot was taken. The coroner said he died of malnutrition, but his close friends called foul play when we interviewed them. Said he got himself a female sous-chef he's been working endless hours with, but no one seems to know how to reach her. And none of their descriptions of this mysterious woman match."

"How'd you get all this information? Were you going to look into Zander's case too? Before bringing me here, I mean?" Julia asked, passing the folder over to her father. She gave Quincy a look of concern, wondering if he was privy to this investigation beforehand.

"I had no idea," Quincy said, as if he read Julia's mind while scanning the photos. "I talked to Victor about bringing you on to another research project his department is conducting."

"Just like how the leaves of a tree benefit from the nutrients gathered by its roots tucked deep in the earth, the departments upstairs don't always know where the food from downstairs comes from."

"What do you think is going on?" Julia asked, in part wanting to find out what Victor's views were founded on. She also wasn't in a rush to share her vision with a complete stranger.

"I know it's not a rabid case of malnutrition going around. This man was a cook, for heaven's sake," Victor said, receiving the folder as Quincy passed it over. "I'm conducting this interview, by the way. I want to know what you know."

Julia paused for a moment and glanced over at Quincy. After receiving a slight nod, Julia told Victor everything she had experienced so far, starting with her first day at The Pit and her second day of county-sponsored nosebleeds. She mentioned Libby Yolke, the beautiful woman with long locks flowing past her shoulders who smelled like lavender and inspired the taste of honey on her tongue. She told him about her nightmare, which she had later categorized as a mental hijacking gone wrong after a second attempt happened moments before she found out about Zander's murder. She finished by describing the woman's true face, the face of a monster.

Victor Jefferson looked undisturbed by Julia's illogical story, like a man who's seen a lot of shit or believes most of what he hears to be BS. Then he tapped the spine of the folder on the desk twice in excitement and radiant enthusiasm.

"Looks like you *are* in the right place at the right time," Victor said, then quickly glanced at Quincy as if a silent message of approval was passed. "You two follow me."

The three traveled toward the elevator near the entrance of the corridor. Victor kept silent as he walked past the opened doors of various scholars and theologians getting ready for the day ahead. It did not surprise Julia when Victor used his ID card to call for the elevator when they reached the end of the hall. This place was locked down tight! When he used it again to force the machine to take them down, her heart jumped, wondering if she was ready for what she had signed up for.

"Your father came to me thinking you could help us with some research we are about to go public with," Victor said, walking between the father-and-daughter pair as they made their way to the basement. "Since the 1700s, citizens of Cardinal-Wood have been no strangers to unexplainable events or patterns."

"You mean like a cat the size of a Mini Cooper."

"Just hear him out, Julia," Quincy said as Victor paused, keeping his focus on the crack of the elevator door. Victor was clearly not amused by Julia's statement.

"The source of these phenomena went undetected until the rise of quantum physics. We had to look deeper for the cause, to find the right wave, frequency, or particle that could be affecting, resonating with, Cardinal-Wood's ecosystem. After decades of research, we've discovered a particle almost as invisible as the dark matter of space. It's called the Axiom Particle." Victor glanced over at Julia as her eyebrows rose with the tide of enlightenment. The elevator stopped its descent and the doors pulled open, exposing a laboratory cloaked in a blinding light.

Julia and Quincy followed Victor out of the elevator into the enormous open space. They were greeted by clicks from lab techs focused on the computer screens of their workstations, ringing alarms from equipment lining the walls, and smoke building up from the far end of the room accompanied by the bursting spray of a fire extinguisher.

"What do these *Axiom* Particles have to do with the monster on a murder spree?"

"Everything, Julia. Technology gave us the opportunity to study something invisible to the naked eye. With the changes you're experiencing, one could hope you're able to provide more insight into the unseen."

"That sounds like a stretch. I don't even know what's going on with me, let alone how to control whatever it is. It's more of a reflex right now," Julia said, remembering when that reflex had failed to react and kick her out of that vision of Zander's murder like a doctor tapping a nonresponsive knee.

"You're a member of the A.R.A's Shadow Department now, where all things done in darkness come to light. You'll figure it out."

*Where all things done in darkness come to light.* Julia hung on those words as they hooked onto images of glowing pupils from Libby's victims and prey trapped inside her memory. Zander, Kyle, Bianca, even chef Carter Smith and his friends, may be caught in Libby's web. Doubts about how to stop Libby had not outweighed her desire to do so until now. The pressure settled onto her shoulders as she realized she probably was the only one who could.

"How can I help?" Julia asked, ready to face the unknown.

"First, we need a sample of your blood. The nosebleeds you and any other visitor to Cardinal-Wood experience are the first sign of assimilation. We have to study your bloodstream to see how the Axiom particles are bonding to your cells and to see if they match anyone else on file or have a completely new genetic makeup."

"So you get my blood and I get access to a secret lab. I'm liking the perks of this job already," Julia said sarcastically as she followed Victor.

"It's a part of those indoctrination papers you were lucky to not have to sign. All A.R.A employees have to give us a sample for research purposes. We even get volunteers from the community at times."

"They even have mine on ice back there," Quincy chimed in, attempting to ease Julia's nerves.

Victor led Julia over to a technician's desk with Quincy trailing behind. The woman seemed to click the keys to her keyboard in sync with the trio as they walked forward, stopping once Victor stood over her computer. Her brunette hair was in a tight bun, tilting back as she looked up from her computer with safety glasses covering her eyes. Behind her workstation was a wall of clear refrigerator units. Rows and rows of vials of blood filled the unit's shelves, each with its own label too small for Julia to read.

"Can you please take her blood and begin the archival process?" Victor asked the technician, who nodded. She took a key from her lab coat, unlocking a drawer at her desk filled with packaged vials and syringes. Julia took a seat at an extra chair in the nameless scientist's workspace and stretched her arm out.

"You said the particles binding to my cells was the first step of assimilation. What's the second?" Julia asked, directing her question toward Victor.

"An awakening of the spirit. Gifts the known logical world can't explain. I'm bringing you onto this team because you have expressed the capacity to see beyond the veil of this physical plane, heightened senses or an elevated discernment of sorts. And by luck or by design, you've not ended up as the third victim in my city after encountering whatever is using Cardinal-Wood as its hunting ground," Victor said as the technician stuck the syringe into Julia's arm with more force than she expected.

"I'm guessing not everyone experiences this awakening or you'd have more agents in the field than scientists in a lab," Julia said, causing the lab tech to lift her head away from the blood pouring into the vial and give Julia a dry stare before she glanced back down.

Victor chuckled. "No, yours is certainly unique. As we are uncovering more of the building blocks of our own world, who knows if they can build bridges to others? The agents deployed upstairs are for cases divided by the line of explanation between science and spirituality. Down here is where the line gets blurred. Doesn't matter. Only furthering the knowledge of truth does. Your studies in criminal forensics and psychology make you the perfect candidate for the first Shadow Department agent, an agent of truth."

Julia let her new title sink in as the technician slid the needle out of her arm. It was like landing on her feet after getting spun around in a tornado. With a firm foundation and her adrenaline pumping, Julia was ready to chase the beast.

Quincy watched as the lab tech bandaged the needle prick on Julia's arm. He stood in silence as his daughter made a decision she believed was her own. Victor's sales pitch regarding the Shadow Department had grown more refined over the years, along with the technology that supported his mission. Quincy remembered the first time he had heard it: the brazen talk of a world undiscovered, of creatures peeking through the veil covering the natural world, and of building blocks of life unturned.

Before leaving Cardinal-Wood for the military with Marie by his side, Quincy was a young man with no direction in a relationship with someone who needed an anchor. He suggested Marie go talk to a professional about the visions she was experiencing. The sessions were going fine for a month or two until Marie came home upset one day. She walked into their apartment holding a card with her face tight in an attempt to contain the tears pushing their way through her puffy eyes. Marie complained and cried about how her current therapist supposedly took another client in her time slot. Her replacement therapist, a male in his early thirties, only left Marie with a card and told her to come back the next day.

*A.R.A.* was inscribed on the front side of the card in gold lettering. On the back was a name: Victor Jefferson. Maybe it was rage at the therapist's office for putting his wife of two years through the insurance maze of network providers, or perhaps it was the simplicity of the card that neither helped Marie nor provided more information for Quincy.

The next day Quincy found himself at the therapist's office next to his wife as she pointed out the strange man occupying her former therapist's seat. Quincy threatened to sue the practice for running a scam on the vulnerable and weak.

"Wouldn't you like to know the truth about her condition—and yours?" Victor rebutted calmly. Curiosity substituted itself for Quincy's rage, causing him and Marie to follow Victor to the original Axiom Research Agency building, a nondistinctive warehouse near Quantico surrounded by the farms and fields of Cardinal-Wood's Heathland district.

"Hey, Dad?" Julia, who now stood in front of Quincy, called out, bringing him back into the present. "I gotta go back upstairs to my phone."

"Alright, baby girl. I'm right behind you."

"Okay," Julia said, a shield of confidence radiating from her smile as she went toward the elevator.

"I'll notify you if anything comes up that you should know," Victor said, directing his voice at Quincy while keeping his eyes on the technician handling the vial of Julia's blood.

"I know you will, Victor. I know you will," Quincy said, glancing back at Julia.

In a rush to reply to Bianca's text and say she'd be back at The Pit tomorrow, Julia missed the label with her name and age being placed on the vial of her blood.

Adrenaline coursed through her veins, pushing her to take action. Her tunnel vision for the task ahead hid answers that could straighten her refracted past.

The lab technician carried Julia's blood sample to the fridge containing hundreds of specimens. She placed the sample between two test tubes of blood labeled with Quincy Thurman and Marie Thurman's names. Quincy followed Julia once the container had closed.

How still must the winds be to calm the raging seas constantly turning, shifting, and crashing from the music of the breeze orchestrated by the sun and the moon. The separate waters below move in tune with the firmament above. Since the dawn of time, this ancient beat has tugged and pulled all creatures.

Imagine a snow globe with crashing waves, a sun that rises in the east and sets in the west. Humans carry on each day with configurations set in their hearts, pushing them forward toward fulfillment, only to be enticed along the way, convinced to settle for the equivalent of fool's gold and forfeit their natural birthright. Since the beginning of time, an ancient being has peered into the souls of humans, attempting to pull them toward destruction just as the moon lowers the tide. Many have embraced this gaze with open eyes, hoping there is an easier way to bear meaningful fruit than the road less traveled. This creature from beyond the veil of the physical plane has held many faces and been called many names throughout time around the world. Now, moving through Cardinal-Wood as swiftly as the wind that shuffles the ocean's waves, Libby Yolke, the beast with a shifting face, searched to erode citizens' dominion over their own souls. This otherworldly monster had finally come across one human whose stronghold wouldn't crumble so easily.

# 5

# PASSIONS, DOUBTS, AND THINGS THAT KEEP US UP AT NIGHT

Developed skepticism or possibly natural ignorance exposed itself like rot in a tree, a black, sagging hole outlined by moss with bugs marching in and out, unable to withstand the slit of an axe thrust toward the weakened opening in the form of a question. *Had I ever believed?* Julia asked herself, ripping through her internal tree of doubt at the stump. *Believe what?* Julia's personal interrogation continued as she checked her eyes in her rearview mirror.

Friday, the day after her inauguration at the Axiom Research Agency, Julia's black Altima was nestled in The Pit's parking lot, positioned to see the entrance and a Wendy's across the street. The sun had risen without a cloud in its way that morning, but Julia couldn't focus on what was ahead or on the nature around her before dissecting herself a little further.

Julia inspected her eyes, searching for any seeds of doubt, before walking into The Pit. A ray of light flashed over her pupils, causing her heart to beat out of rhythm until the sun rose a little further, shifting the glare. Julia closed the mirror, sounding off a frustrated clap as the plastic cover shut. What was she searching for, anyway? Why was she so eager to chase a spirit, a ghost, or whatever Libby called itself, a creature that hid in the shadows of the natural world? The only answer that constantly repeated over the broadcast of her conscience was that she *never believed.* The opportunity to confront this hidden unbelief, to disprove the doubts tucked in her soul, waited in the building ahead.

Throughout the years, Quincy would send back recorded CDs of his sermons whenever he deployed for months at a time. Julia listened to them at night before bed in her headphones and CD player before MP3s and Bluetooth became a thing. Words about a creator, unconditional love, even everlasting life would soothe her spirit to sleep. One sermon, however, kept Julia awake through the night, curled on her bed under the covers.

*"We battle not with flesh and blood but against principalities and spirits..."*

Night after night, shadows morphed, taking on new shapes as the breeze shook the tree outside of Julia's window. The only way to prevent a full insomniac conversion after hearing about a fight taking place involving her and opponents invisible to the eye was to downsize the fear, to turn it into a fantasy the size of Santa Claus.

As customers straggled into The Pit to grab either a breakfast sandwich before work or a simple black coffee, Julia laughed at her juvenile ignorance that led her to believe the only time to fear invisible warriors was during the night. With her own eyes, Julia had confirmed the existence of Libby was a fact. She could even be one of the customers walking into The Pit right now. Fear is powerful enough to make the impossible appear to be a problem. And faith is the fuel that pushes humans through the impossible.

Julia exited her car to head inside as well. What other creatures beside Libby Yolke use Earth as their backyard? Can enter through a door outside of human perception with dominion over anyone or anything on its property? She stopped her thoughts from drifting down a highway of hypotheticals, letting out a sigh in front of The Pit.

A black Challenger parked at the Wendy's across the street caught Julia's attention, infusing her eyebrows with curiosity. With an elbow hanging outside of the driver's window, a conspicuous man sporting a suit and tie while sunglasses covered his eyes dragged a breakfast sandwich up to his mouth. Julia walked over to the car as Detective Bullaby's sunglasses shuffled with each bite.

"Morning, Detective. I see there's no shame in eating on the job," Julia said, leaning against the Challenger.

"Please get off the car. It's police property and just been detailed." Bullaby took another bite. Crumbs of bread sprinkled onto his beard. Bullaby wiped his mouth as he chewed, sending the crumbs down to his blazer.

"Is that so?" Julia responded, lifting herself from the car as the crumbs fell to the floor while Bullaby patted his chest clean. "Out of all the flavored heart attacks, you chose to eat at the Wendy's across the street from The Pit. I'm surprised to see one of Cardinal-Wood's finest staking out the place after my cousin's death was ruled a suicide."

Bullaby's head shook from side to side. He chewed his food faster to make room to speak. He cleared his throat with a grunt, assisted by his last sip of cartoned orange juice. "Just enjoying some breakfast, ma'am. My condolences to you and your family regarding Zander. But you're right. His case is closed and we aren't looking into his death any further."

"Do you believe the autopsy report?" Julia asked, leaning forward to hear his response, as if it was going to be a secret between the two.

"Doesn't matter what I believe. We both watched the same security footage."

Julia opened her mouth but stopped herself from giving Detective Bullaby the indoctrination speech she had heard from Victor Jefferson the day before about a world undiscovered by our natural eyes, or from explaining how belief skews perception. That was a lesson too fresh to share as Julia was in the middle of processing it herself. "Enjoy the rest of your breakfast," Julia replied instead with a plastic smirk. She gave the car two taps before walking away.

Bullaby took another bite of his breakfast sandwich. "If you see anything suspicious in there, remember I'm just three numbers away."

Julia glanced back. *How could he help with what he refuses to see?* She noticed Bullaby reach for his orange juice and toss it to the floor after realizing the container was empty.

"Dammit." Julia heard Bullaby's cry to the heavens, covered by bacon, eggs, and bread as she crossed the street to The Pit.

Julia walked into a cloud of lavender filling The Pit's waiting room like a low morning fog. The sweet scent lacked the strength to steal Julia's resolve from the task ahead but permeated the room as if an animal had marked its territory. Julia pushed forward, shaking her head to remove any lingering self-doubt.

A young woman stood behind the podium, waiting to greet all incoming customers for the day. Beautiful in her own way, the woman, who looked a few years younger than Julia, smiled as Julia approached. Green rubber bands latched onto braces lined the hostess's teeth and braids clanked against her glasses as she tilted her head with a wave.

Disappointed Kyle wasn't in front of her, but relieved she wasn't walking toward someone displaying ethereal beauty or a glow in their eyes, Julia found it hard to reciprocate the wave. In turn, she greeted the hostess with a smirk and a nod. Kyle, the most heartbroken of The Pit's employees over Zander's death, was Julia's first prospect to interview regarding Libby. His outrage during the initial questioning from Bullaby was layered with sincerity, as if he had lost a brother too. This notion was either a hunch or plain hope that his grief could be used as a wedge to sever the hold Libby had over him.

"Um, I mean, I'm sorry for your loss," the hostess said as Julia passed, stopping her just before the large red curtain. "He was awesome to work with. Always had good energy," Tiffany said while Julia studied the name tag pinned to her black-and-red vest.

"Thank you." Julia turned her smirk into a smile designed to greet empathy or pity with open arms. She took a step forward. "Is Kyle in today?" Julia asked, stopping herself before crossing into the dining area.

Tiffany looked around to see if anyone else could hear what she was about to say. "He hasn't been in all week. Supposedly he's not returning Bianca's calls either. Some of us think he's on the run, in on it somehow."

Julia's eyebrows raised in sarcastic shock. "Really? Why would people think that?"

"Oh, my god. Not only was he a creep, but actually creepy, if you understand what I mean. He hit on every female working here and, if you walked by during slow hours, you could catch him staring off into nothing or drawing on napkins." Tiffany rambled on, shaking her head in disgust. "Too much mixed energy. Introvert and extrovert. No stability." She finished, untucking a necklace that hung under her shirt and rubbing a crystal at its end.

"I'll keep that in mind." Julia hesitated to ask her next question. "Do you know where he lives?"

"Sadly, yeah. He text-bombed everyone here the address to his uncle's mansion, inviting us to a party. You want it?" Tiffany asked, her eyebrows curled with disturbed curiosity.

"Yeah. I know he and Zander were close. Just want to check up on him."

"Oh, that's nice." Tiffany responded, softening her face in approval. "I knew I liked your vibe when you walked in. Something genuine, very unique about you." Tiffany said, rubbing her crystal one more time before scrolling through her phone.

"So, his uncle has a mansion?" Julia asked as Tiffany searched her messages.

"Yeah, he lives with him up in Amada Grove among the other Cardinal-Wood royalty. Brags about how he's gonna be a millionaire when the old man croaks because they're the last two in the family. Found it. Here you go." Tiffany showed Julia her phone.

Between scanning texts with responses ranging from *fuck off* to *I'll be there in the group chat*, Julia finally came across the address. "Thank you for this," Julia said, typing the address into the notes app of her phone. "Can I see his number too?"

"No problem, girl. Slide mine in there too. If you ever need to talk to some-one, ya know."

Julia took both numbers down. *Why not?*

Customers sprinkled around the dining area enjoyed their breakfasts with eyes glued either onto their phones or each other. Some chatted about sports. "*I can't believe I put money on those bums.*" Others read up on current events between sips of coffee. "*Fucking inflation.*" The rest took photos of food or themselves to post on social media. "*What tags should I add?*" None seemed affected by the lav-ender aroma circulating the room. Julia couldn't shake the feeling she was walking straight into the monster's mouth.

"My nephew ordered some of his food online and said it tasted like it came from heaven," an older man seated at the bar said, pointing to the TVs hanging over the rows of alcohol. Julia stopped before crossing into the kitchen as a picture of Carter Smith flashed on the screen. His bright red hair contrasted with the white chef's uniform in the photograph. Carter had a radiant smile as he stood over a dozen strawberry, lemon, and chocolate cupcakes—the last meal he ever made.

The image was more crisp and curated than the stills from Carter's IG live session Julia had seen at the A.R.A. The filters used for the photo made the cup-cakes pop with color that could easily make any viewer salivate. No doubt this photo made the cut to his profile page to attract customers. Even looking at the picture from a TV screen, Julia saw the flash in Carter's eyes, brighter than a glare.

"I hope his family eventually finds peace," Julia said.

The older man raised his cup of coffee with a nod. "Amen to that."

*"This was the first of two ruled suicides in the Empire Estate apartment building, within seven days of each other. Zander Thurman was discovered unresponsive in his room Monday of this week,"* a blonde news anchor in a blue dress reported. With regal posture, the anchorwoman posed for the camera with a stern look as a photo of Zander appeared on the screen.

Zander sat at his desk slightly, turned away from the computer, smiling while he faced the camera. Possibly Julia's aunt or uncle had taken the picture, happy to see their son working on his passion. Or maybe it was a friend excited to take a behind-the-scenes photo. After a few blinks, Julia knew for a fact that Zander's pupils were missing the light held by all the victims entranced by Libby. Immediately a new idea electrified her body.

*"Mental health experts in Cardinal-Wood are worried this may be a trend in the wrong direction for the young entrepreneurs and content creators in the area, dome say the world."* The anchorwoman finished, giving the audience another fierce stare.

Eggs sprinkled with pepper fried on skillets as servers refilled pots of coffee back in the kitchen. Under the zing from spiced pepper cracking on the skillet and dark roast steaming from multiple pots, the lavender aroma reached Julia's nose like a scent left over from the kitchen's last deep clean.

Most of these faces were still unfamiliar to Julia, as it was only her second day on the job. *Has anyone else come across Libby? Is she here right now?* She scanned the faces of her coworkers with each step. She passed a closed door leading into Bianca's office on her way to the break room.

Julia entered the employee area behind the kitchen and sat down in front of a vacant locker. There wasn't a good explanation for her to be back here. She carried her debit card, a maxed-out credit card, and her ID in the cardholder of her phone case—nothing large to stow away. Her purse was in the car. Julia repositioned the hair behind her ear with a trembling hand.

The Libby pheromone spread around the building had a suffocating effect separate from its entrancing properties. Julia wondered if her new gift from Cardinal-Wood was to blame as she stilled her hand, resting it back on her lap. Elevated senses and heightened discernment allowed her to perceive the poisonous spores floating from room to room, hitting her lungs as harsh as a methane leak with each breath. Maybe this was the cost of fighting the enchantment, the price of knowing. Julia needed time to calm her thumping heart and to silence her mind. Constantly avoiding Libby's hooks from sinking into her soul was a task she had to grow into. The pulsating heartbeat pounding through Julia's eardrums eased after a few deep breaths.

"Hello, new girl. Welcome back," a nasal yet familiar voice called out from behind her.

The throbbing in Julia's eardrum ramped up again as the room exploded, filling with the lavender toxin. She turned around slowly as Libby's true face, with razor-sharp teeth digging into Zander's skull, flashed in her mind.

Bobby stood at the entrance with a grin and beams shining from his eyes like two searchlights. Something was different. Something about his appearance had been distorted in a way that made Julia's stomach curl as she tried to figure it out. *Is he taller now?*

"Good morning, Bobby," Julia said in a slow cadence. Bobby replied with a soft wave.

Bobby took a few steps toward Julia, causing her to turn her back to him again and concentrate on her breathing. The stench similar to what Julia thought the bubonic plague smelled like wasn't leaking from Bobby's armpits anymore. The source of the lavender spores floating around The Pit was right behind her, oozing out of his pores! Julia closed her eyes and counted to three in her head, taking a deep breath with each number. 1... 2... 3... and she opened them after configuring a new baseline for her body's stress threshold. With disregard to the poison populating the area like a plumber dealing with a faulty sump pump in a hole full of shit and piss, focusing on the job would get Julia to clean air faster.

"How's your family holding up?" Bobby asked, directing the question toward Julia but paying more attention to what his thumb was scrolling through on his phone.

Julia looked at Bobby as he stood next to her in front of a locker containing a black backpack she assumed he owned. Insight stilled the response on her lips. Compared to her first night shadowing Bobby around The Pit, he had definitely grown taller. His posture was perfect now, with shoulders as rigid as mountains. It was magical turnaround from the slouching, frail man Julia had met on Sunday.

"We're, uh, we're taking it day by day," Julia answered, studying Bobby more closely after her rehearsed response. He continued to be overtly invested in his phone rather than Julia's words. The illumination from Bobby's phone screen revealed his smooth face. The red polka dot acne that plagued his profile had been erased.

*But how?* Bobby's *He's All That* makeover looked like it had happened on a cellular rather than a cosmetic level. Cheekbones cut like a model's allowed the shadows left in the room to accent Bobby's perfect jawline. His hair was trimmed and greased. The sweat swamp that once dampened his scalp had been dried. Even with the lack of perspiration, Bobby's skin had a vibrant glow.

"That's good to hear," Bobby said, ending his scripted sympathy. He paused for a moment, squinting down at his phone screen. "My boy-toy trainer canceled on me after one session. Now I have to ad-lib a workout when I go. Must've not liked how I was hitting on him between reps." He stuffed his phone in his pocket, letting out a deep sigh as he shook his head. "First world problem, I guess." Bobby rolled his shimmering pupils like a full moon passing through a cloudy night sky, then reached for the backpack in the locker.

"Hey, did the cops ever interview you?" Julia asked, now on her feet with soles firmly planted on ground invisible to the human eye because of her new gift. What occurrences or minor details had Julia missed in the hours before her awakening? She now knew about the lavender toxins that entranced and the taste of honey that enticed. The glowing eyes acted like a barcode attached to a product. Libby causing this chaos was a fact, but Julia still didn't know all the symptoms of those she—*it*—affected. She believed a breadcrumb toward the truth was in front of her.

Bobby hesitated as he unzipped his bag and then proceeded until the zipper's cadence ceased. "You wanna know who I told them I saw Zander leave with?" Bobby asked, pulling out a bottle of vitamins with a smirk that grew goosebumps on Julia's forearms.

"You asked me why I kept calling Libby a woman when I spoke about her—*its*—lavender perfume. My head was a little too cloudy to argue what I thought then was an absolute fact. So, who did you see?" Julia asked, taking a step closer to Bobby.

Bobby's grin widened as he dropped two pills into his hand and twisted the lid closed.

"Omega-3," Bobby said, shaking the pill bottle. "Helps with brain health and head fog," he said, pushing out each word between bites of the chewable vitamins. He put the container back in his bag and zipped it closed. "I told the cops Zander left alone."

*Be careful who you talk to because you never know if one of their demons is speaking for them.* A personal code of ethics Julia had adopted during her high school days demanded to be revisited. She had attended three schools in four years, one of which was in Japan. A lot of unique interactions took place during those times, in the age range when people's villain story can originate, turning them into either a dictator or a humanitarian based off the weight of the trauma experienced in the halls of raging hormones. People lie. That's a fact Julia held true before any cafeteria politics came into play. Whether it was something petty like Susan Mathews in the third grade, who claimed Julia called Elizabeth Drew *ugly* so Susan could play on Elizabeth's kickball team instead of Julia, or Marie drinking and smoking herself to death just to avoid telling Julia key details of her past and possibly to avoid confronting the truth herself. A lie of omission is still a lie. And our demons puppeteer us toward destruction.

*Am I even speaking to Bobby?* Julia's face tightened as she squinted, attempting to gaze deeper than the glowing pupils in front of her. "There's no way the cops bought that. We all gave a description." Julia said, hoping Bobby wasn't privy to the lack of video evidence.

"The two detectives I spoke to weren't disturbed by my statement at all. They seemed relieved, actually. Something told me, I mean, I got a sense that what I saw fit with what they already *believed* to be true."

*Bullshit.*

Shame or confusion are the principal ingredients of deception, but why lie? Bobby's magical makeover empowered the once sweaty and slouching body-conscious waiter past all insecurities. His composed demeanor fit around his body like a lawyer's tailored suit. He was armed with a smile and charm that acted like a bulletproof vest.

"Did you talk to the cops before or after your miraculous healing?" Julia asked without watering down her sarcasm.

Bobby tilted his face toward the centerpiece mirror that hung in all the lockers and rubbed his thumb across the unblemished skin of his chin. "I woke up that morning splashing in puddles of sweat on my bed. Dropped thirty pounds in one night. I felt light. Free." He turned back toward Julia and adjusted his red vest. "Hit my head on the shower rod. Found out I grew five inches too. Went the whole day without an extra drop of sweat or having to change my shirt. The only thing that fell from my body throughout the day were my pimples and zits. Fell off like dried scabs, scattered around my apartment like a trail of raisins. Shit looked nasty. But I felt good. Looked better than good! Imagine waking up from a living nightmare into a dream you've always wanted."

Marie Thurman's sitcom smile melting away, morphing into the Libby–Marie hybrid of Julia's own nightmare, replayed in her head. The idea that she had experienced a failed mental hijacking of sorts was formed out of fear, a feeling that part of her had been stolen overnight or at least a gash in her heart had been exposed. And Julia only felt the pain after waking like how a broken bone sends fire ringing through the body once eyes catch a femur protruding from the skin.

What if Libby offered a symbiotic gift instead of a parasitic curse? Julia's chest tightened as rapid short breaths passed through her nostrils. Would Julia have taken the deal if she knew the terms of the agreement? The cliff that Libby brought Julia to in her mind's eye. What would she have received if she had made that metaphorical leap? Would time go backward? Would the dead be resurrected? Desires of her heart Julia thought she had tucked away in a deep corner of her soul bled out.

"Ahh, you've seen what dream you can have, haven't you? What could be your gift? It's never too late," Bobby said as the sparks in his eyes danced.

The concept of perfection plagues the spirit that knows the status is impossible to achieve. Fairy tales or fantasy fiction had never been enjoyable to Julia—the escapism of an elaborate story pulling you to another world only to blink once you turn the page, dragging you back to reality and realize your mother is snoring on the couch with a lit cigarette in her hand. There's no natural way to stitch the internal wounds of neglect and lack of self-worth, or to remove the thought that your presence was the catalyst for your mother's depression. Libby couldn't give Julia anything she didn't believe existed. The truth was that none of Marie Thurman's demise was Julia's fault.

"Let me know when you're ready to talk, new girl. *I'm* always willing to listen," Bobby said, finishing with a smile. He went toward the exit, bumping shoulders with Julia as he passed.

Physical contact between the two changed the frequency of Julia's visual perception as if she had peeked at an X-ray of Bobby's soul. Down the bright tunnels of his pupils, which led to the desires of one's heart, Julia found herself viewing a borderless space covered in darkness. In the center of this void was a floating mirror encased in a gold frame. The void offered nothing for the mirror to reflect, but a silhouette began to form. Bobby, without his supernatural makeover, was trapped in his sweat-stained work uniform on the slab of glass. He was roaming from left to right and right to left, out of the frame to right back in. He was further back from the focal point, as if he were standing in the distance to press his face against the mirror, smearing sweat across the surface in an inaudible panic. No sound pulsated through the void as Bobby banged on the mirror. No voice rang out of the frame as he cried out for help.

A hideous mouth with cracked grey scales for lips and rows of sword-like teeth rose across the horizon of the void. An alligator's grin hung over the mirror, encasing Bobby with the same enthusiasm Julia imagined the prehistoric creature had every time it dragged a gazelle distracted by quenching its own thirst into the deep.

"Hey, welcome back, Julia!" Bianca came to the entrance of the employee lounge. Julia's vision returned to the present moment, igniting a throbbing pain in her temples. Bianca stood at the threshold radiating with pleasure, similar to any manager who catches their employees slacking on the job. She waved Bobby over to her as he rubbed the side of his head. By the wincing on Bobby's face, Julia imagined he was feeling the same metaphorical aluminum bat pounding against his head.

"What did you just do to me?" Bobby asked with some bass in his voice. The lights in his eyes flashed brightly, like flicking on and off the high beams of a car.

"Resolve your problems on your own time. Not the time I'm paying you for. Bobby, table six is looking for you." Bianca turned to walk away, but stopped to make sure Bobby followed.

Bobby left Julia with a smirk. "See you around, new girl." He went around Bianca into the kitchen.

"I need you out there too, Julia. You can take some time off still if you're not up for a busy day," Bianca stated as sparks in her pupils danced in harmony.

Julia shook her head. "No, I'm fine. Right now keeping busy at work is the best thing for me to do."

Common ground between humans and beasts that roam the air, prowl the Earth, or swim in the sea is nature. Cause and effect act as judge, jury, and executioner. A squirrel chasing a rolling nut into a busy street will surely get run over. The migration of birds exchanging cold climates for hotter days is nothing more than a winter vacation in Tulum. A starving fox in the woods attracts a pack of vultures to hover, waiting to consume death. A drug dealer living in a low-end apartment will lace dope with poison just to stretch out the supply only to pay the water bill by selling to an addict whose outstretched hand doesn't know it's their last fix.

Julia loved making connections between humans and the rest of the animal kingdom. The only things separating us from them are higher brain function and opposable thumbs. What if we never saw a bird fly? Would there be planes? If no one ever saw a lizard grow its tail back, would the medical field have been able to provide enhanced prosthetics? Social media has exposed the human hive mind. Millions of small interest groups spread across the Internet, connecting like-minded individuals who will swarm against any offense taken against their chosen hill to die on, much like a grasshopper invading an ant mound.

That's why Julia couldn't escape the feeling she was in the middle of her own wildlife documentary. *Watch as the trees constrict on the lone bruin as she strolls into enemy territory. A wolf pack dead ahead!* Julia narrated to herself with the worst Steve Irwin impersonation ever. On the surface Julia was the bear surrounded by snarling teeth leaking with drool and growls directed by eyes filled with constellations. Bobby and Bianca, even the corpses of Zander and Carter, circled around her, reminding Julia how impossible the task at hand may be.

Throughout the day Bobby and Bianca avoided Julia, who was stationed behind the bar. Bianca reasoned to Julia that making drinks would be easier to handle on her first day back and only her second day on the job. Once Julia took her post among the tequilas and taps, she realized too late that she'd been trapped in a cage. Bianca disappeared for hours, retreating to her office. No eye contact came from Bobby, who bounced around the dining area modeling his sculpted features for the customers. Any drink orders he placed came from the auxiliary register at the far end of the room.

*What did I see? Seriously, what the fuck was that about?* Julia repeatedly asked herself as she observed Bobby's enchanted charisma eclipse the room. Hours went by as she tried to rationalize the void she had peeked into, comparing the Bobby she had perceived pleading for his life against the present version captivating the guests. The only explanation on *how she saw what she saw,* one that made use of the current known variables of Julia's complex life equation, was that her Cardinal-Wood awakening was ongoing. The fusion of the Axiom particles and her blood wasn't complete, and there was no way to guess how her elevated senses would manifest themselves next, or if she'd be able to control them.

Where could that mirrored prison be? Based on the current Bobby's reaction back in the employee room, it was somewhere Julia wasn't supposed to see. *"Imagine waking up from a living nightmare into a dream you've always wanted."*

Julia focused on the Bobby she saw trapped in the mirror, steadying her hand while mixing the ingredients for a rum-rock beach order. Bobby was pudgy, smearing sweat across the mirror as his fist banged against the glass. The acne spread across his face tucked between the creases of flesh formed by fear.

"Excuse me? Hello?" A slender and tall man with Tom Cruise–like features, black hair, blue eyes, and an action-figure chin, called for Julia's attention. She splashed the last drop of coke into the drink mix as she looked up and slid the drink down the bar for a faceless waiter to pick up. Fifty-two drink combinations were locked in her mind but she still couldn't put faces to the names of the fifteen servers working during her shift.

"What can I get you, sir?" Julia asked, hiding the disdain employees have when required to complete the tasks they're paid for throughout the day.

"Uh, I need your help." The man sporadically glanced over his shoulder toward the dining area. "Can you give my number to that waiter over there?" the man asked, pushing a card into Julia's fingers. His eyes were following Bobby around the room like a fish drawn to a squirming worm on an invisible hook. "My husband can't seem to take his eyes off him either, but I dunno; I want him to myself. I mean, can you blame me? Just look at him. You think you can do that for me?" The man pleaded, lining his voice with a whimper.

Julia's interest in men had been explored and long forgotten, but it wasn't hard to see Bobby as desirable. Did Libby take Bobby to a mental cliff as well and present him with the body of his dreams? Did she promise him all the recognition, love, and lust entrusted to only the most beautiful and say all he had to do was give up his mind? No. His soul.

Every decision is made to serve a purpose, consciously or subconsciously. The hyperhidrosis-stricken, acne-ridden, body-odor bomb of an employee at The Pit, Bobby, would have loved to have experienced a day without profusely sweating. Throw in a free total makeover and you'd find it hard for anyone to refuse. But the deal wasn't free at all. Bobby just didn't know the cost. The image of Bobby trapped in the void of his soul within a mirror's frame sprinted across Julia's memory. She lightly scratched the base of her throat as a random tic, attempting to maintain composure.

"No problem. I'll find the right time to hand this to him for you," Julia said, feigning a smile as she inspected the card before stuffing it into her pocket. Brad Steinbeck, Attorney at Law, nodded as he mouthed a thank you and then dismissed himself. Brad navigated his way back to his table, unable to tame his excitement. His smile grew bigger and bigger with each step and he even attempted to get Bobby's attention with a short wave. Bobby projected a politician's charm. Julia could see the grin and glowing eyes from the bar as Brad rejoined his husband. His significant other looked none too pleased with Brad's flirting as his own face began to boil red all the way up to his blonde bowl cut.

Julia's throat tightened as her breath tried to keep pace with her thoughts. If Libby was a part of an animal kingdom from a realm undiscovered, what would its Earth counterpart be? All signs pointed to one of the most hostile reproductive sequences nature had to offer, one that even in this moment flipped Julia's stomach left and right the same way it had when her hobby had first led her down a rabbit hole to this discovery—the wasp.

A leaf deep in the woods being nibbled away by a green caterpillar camouflaged on its surface sends an invisible wave out into the air as a cry for help. Soon a lone buzzing hero answers the call and swoops in to sting the caterpillar in the act. The wasp's sting doesn't kill the once feasting caterpillar; no, in fact, the caterpillar will carry on as if nothing had happened and even finish its meal, but now it's eating for a dozen more. The wasp's sting injected its larvae into the caterpillar, leaving it with a gift of conversion before destruction and turning the caterpillar into a host, an incubator for the wasp's children. As it eats, they grow. Zombified maternal instincts kick in and the caterpillar protects itself in the interest of its adopted children, waiting for them to burst out from inside when the time has come. Still the caterpillar survives the larvae seeping in between the cracks of its cells and holds its post as the maternal protector until the grubs hatch from their cocoons.

How about the emerald jewel wasp, which aims for a roach's head when it stings, disabling the insect's dopamine production to negate any acts of free will? Then the emerald thief rips out one of the roach's antennae for a five-hour energy drink of blood and proceeds to lay its larvae in the zombified host.

Could the desires of one's heart act like such a calling card for Libby's services? Zander's YouTube dreams had been drained away by the jaws of a monster that pierced his brain with precision. What could that *thing* have offered Bianca, who had been barricaded in her office for the past six hours? Was Libby feeding off of Bobby, or was she waiting to fatten him up like a pig, allowing him to draw more victims into her web? Zander was used as bait for the eyes that caught Libby's gaze a few days ago. Was the monster's dopamine drone network constantly expanding in the same way, waiting days and counting minutes until *it* collected *its* prize? If so, Libby had reserves of food around the world, millions of people willing to be her next meal.

The walls of the dining area slowly inched their way closer, folding in on Julia like origami during the last hour of her shift. Libby's pheromones and poisonous spores spread around the guests enjoying their meals, men and women dazzled by Bobby floating around the room. Who was the beast going to court next? Would *it* meet them at The Pit? Julia didn't think it would be a good idea to wait around and find out. She wouldn't know what to do if she actually faced that *thing*! All she knew was that she needed some fresh air and to check on Kyle. She needed to observe all the enchanted employees with her own eyes but there was nothing promising that she'd find anything helpful or, ultimately, discover her own death.

During the drive from Lyn City to Amada Grove, the sun exchanged the blue sky with streaking accented clouds for a purple-hued backdrop. An hour of sitting in traffic allowed Julia to witness the moment when the sun and the moon shared the cosmic stage. The reflective rock took its full shape in the east as the decaying star shrank behind the western horizon. The twenty-story buildings of Lyn City's downtown area shrank along the road toward the northern suburbs. Each structure of brick, steel, or stone Julia passed was smaller than the last as if pulled from a Russian nesting doll. The architectural wizardry transitioned as Julia crossed into Amada Grove. There she saw only grocery stores, one-story strip malls, and houses with acres or pools between them. *Your destination is on the right. 316 Terrace Way.*

Julia's fingers tightened around the steering wheel as she stopped the car. Two roaring lion statues made of stone guarded the driveway's entrance. The road wound up and around a manicured hill to an uninviting house the size of a school. A lone window in the west wing, out of what Julia estimated to be around fifteen, emanated a green-and-orange light. Julia felt as if the mansion was a giant beast sleeping on a mountain with one eye open, waiting to make her its next meal. Julia took her foot off the brake and inched forward.

Moments later Julia found herself standing in front of a red door in the twilight of the day. Her fists were still tightly clenched as if she were holding the steering wheel when she went to ring the doorbell. No sign of movement came from the home, no lights getting cut along the way to the door or yelling from anyone inside about *who was closer.* Julia looked back at the three cars in the driveway, not counting her own. A blue Tesla coated with pollen radiated a green hue. Undisturbed, the particles mixed with the red Honda and black Cadillac, shifting their colors like paint on a pallet.

Just as Julia went to ring the doorbell a second time, she heard the click of the lock. An elderly man with a scruffy bald head, somewhere between seventy and death, opened the door. His glasses hung toward the edge of his nose and age sloped his shoulders. He looked disturbed, wearing a home's number one cozy uniform of slippers, sweats, and a wrinkled white t-shirt as he processed who was standing at the door. His mouth went crooked as if it was snared on the right words to say.

"Good evening, sir, I hope I'm not bothering you, but my name is Jul—."

"Kyle!" the elderly man yelled out. His voice projected like a hoarse megaphone, taxing his vocal cords into a coughing fit. "That woman you've been crying about is here." He finished yelling over his shoulder in between coughs, turned, and waved Julia inside. "Please come in. He's been going on and on about you since his friend passed."

The old man led Julia into a large, dim foyer lit by candles hung on the upper-level wall. Weaving fire danced across the wooded floors, revealing two sets of stairs curving upward on the left and right.

A loud rumbling from upstairs picked up beat like footsteps from a proceeding marching band. *Clang!*

Julia's ankles almost propelled her forward in fright until she heard a distant bowl spinning on the ground like a giant quarter.

"Give him some time. I'll get you some water while you wait," the old man said, walking deeper into the foyer underneath the upstairs landing.

Julia watched the old man inch his way into the abyss he knew as home. He disappeared out of reach of the fire and, to Julia, it looked like the man had been swallowed whole. The stairs on the east and west wings curved like fangs while the candles across the wall flared like each were a pair of eyes from Libby's victims.

"Excuse me? Sir?" Julia called out as she followed him into the unknown.

There was a pause as Julia stood covered in darkness.

"Don't worry, I'm just lookin' for the light." The old man flipped a switch a few inches to the right of Julia. An overhead light shone down on a long ebony table that could seat twenty guests with a thin green cloth running down the middle. Glass panels lined the back wall to highlight the art the man called his backyard. "Follow me. You caught me readin' in the kitchen. And I, uh, I apologize if I kept you waiting at the door." The man turned back with a smile flavored with hope of understanding. "My name's Ledele, but everyone who was alive while they knew me called me Led."

"Nice to meet you, Led. I'm Julia."

"Hold on, Julia, I don't know you yet," Led said, turning his head with a smile acknowledging his own sense of humor. A brief moment of lightheartedness rushed through Julia's body like a cold glass of water as she followed Led down the length of the table. Unplagued by his imminent appointment with death, Led still carried charisma in his social arsenal, a trait Julia welcomed as it loosened the stiffness of her knees.

They passed generations of family portraits along both walls of the room, black-and-white photos of families depicting either a sole child or up to a dozen siblings.

"Just in here," Led said, turning into the kitchen connected to the right of the dining hall. Pots and pans hung from storage rails while stainless steel appliances held their post in the restaurant-sized kitchen. Led handed Julia a cold bottle of water from the fridge.

Julia loosened the airtight seal for a sip. Stagnant air in the house shifted against Julia's neck like something was stalking her from behind, ready to make its move.

"That's not her, Uncle Led," a low-energy voice murmured.

Julia turned around to discover a disheveled Kyle standing behind her wearing a half tucked blue Oxford and khakis along with matching wrinkles running from top to bottom. His pupils shimmered in the shadows of the threshold as a whiff of lavender marched up Julia's nostrils.

"Yo-you smell nothing like her. You look nothing like her." Kyle ran his hand through his unbrushed hair while shaking his head, unable to hide his disappointment. "Please just leave the same way you came in. I'll be in my room, Uncle Led."

"That's no way to talk to your guest, Kyle. Even tho she ain't who ya lookin for don't mean you can't speak," Led said, stopping Kyle as he walked away.

"Kyle, it's me, Julia, Zander's cousin."

"I know who you are, but what are you doing here?" Kyle asked with his back turned. "Did Libby send you?" he asked, peeking over his shoulder.

That question put a theory in Julia's head, one that could hurt her if she let it fester and grow. What if Libby's dopamine drones lacked the capacity to share knowledge like a true hive mind and their only use was to spread the queen bee's seed? Perhaps Libby kept them on a need-to-know basis while they enacted her will. Kyle should have known Julia hadn't joined the colony; he even said so. She smelled nothing like Libby. Julia's untainted pheromones must have smelled like shit to the drones the same way the lavender smell emitting from them made Julia's stomach twist. Julia briefly second-guessed whether to come had been her own decision in the first place or if the lavender particles she had inhaled throughout the day had finally broken through her spirit and Libby was backing her into a corner.

"You remember its name now? You were shooting blanks when the detectives needed answers."

"I found out those weren't my answers to give."

"What do you mean?"

"She speaks to me. Reveals secrets. Says she has big plans for me."

"Kyle, we need to find a way to stop that thing. It's dangerous and it doesn't belong here."

"No! You're wrong. She's right at home. Let me show you."

Kyle slunk toward the stairs. After one glance back at Led, who'd made his way to the reading nook in the corner undisturbed, Julia followed behind Kyle.

The two walked the curved stairs up to the candlelit second floor. Down the hall was a room with green lights and orange pulsating flashes shining through the crack of the door. Julia figured this was the room staring down at her from the street, the eye of the beast.

"Look, it's amazing, right?" Kyle said, pushing the door open with his shoulder.

Being greeted by paint fumes and cum-stained sheets distracted Julia from whatever Kyle wanted her to see. Candles on lampstands illuminated portraits hanging on the wall to the left of the door while green rays shone down from the ceiling lights, revealing a large, studio-sized room. Small bowls of paint and leftover food were spread across the floor. Crumbled napkins and crusty socks peppered the hardwood like a minefield.

Embers dancing across the hanging portraits caught Julia's eye as Kyle walked over to a canvas stationed in the center of the room. She couldn't see what was on the other side of the canvas but she didn't mind. The large self-portraits she figured to be the continued theme of Kyle's family lineage used as interior decor actually held no relation.

Lead markings outlined creases caused by a familiar grin. A few teeth were even showing at the far corner of his smile that resembled the one from his graduation photo. Julia remembered the two of them joking about how he looked like a scamming car salesman. A near-perfect sketch of Zander was on display against the wall.

Caught between breathing and her motor functions failing, Julia gasped for air as she studied the work of art. Pencil marks wriggled on Zander's head as a sign of his signature waves. Even his hairline had a lifelike sharpness. What kept speeding up Julia's heart rate to the point where she was beginning to feel light-headed was the hallowed eyes in the sketch. White holes acted as the centerpieces of Zander's profile as if Kyle had used the blank color of the canvas to highlight the *windows of the soul* for creative reasons, but Julia knew that wasn't true. She inspected the other pieces with the same awe and fear.

Bianca, Bobby, and Kyle (a self-portrait) were included amongst the pantheon of faces hanging on the wall. Each one was crafted with spectacular detail, a testament to Kyle's talent. What Julia had assumed was just a hobby explored during boredom turned out to be a natural gift. Bianca's ponytail had the right number of loose strands of hair flowing over her forehead, similar to how Julia saw her hours before. Heavy-handed pencil marks emphasized the chiseled jawbone of Bobby's mystical makeover.

Two remaining sketches locked the air in Julia's nostrils in place. She focused on the one with her hair, the one that reminded her of the relief she felt each time after successfully pressing her curls down to her shoulders. The eyebrows arched like her banners of *resting bitch face.* Julia's thoughts became trapped in the same prison as her breathing was being held briefly. Where the other sketches had ears, lips, noses, and were missing only eyes, the sketch of Julia was missing them all.

Well, they were not exactly missing, but features Julia didn't recognize as her own were in their place.

A blazing inferno outlined Julia's ears like fiery earmuffs. An object protruded out of the portrait's slightly open mouth, which at first made Julia think it was a snake's tongue until she noticed the small detail depicting light reflecting off the tip of a blade. And the eyes had two shining suns for pupils.

Julia turned to Kyle, who was now kneeling in front of the canvas. His face was partially covered, obstructed by the object that held his gaze. Julia couldn't see what he was looking at but she saw a tear roll down Kyle's cheek just before he started to whimper.

*He's been barricaded in this house, losing his mind.* Julia turned her focus back to the pieces on the wall. She tried to ignore the thoughts that led toward deciphering the meaning of her self-portrait. Still, curiosity tugged. The feeling that her move to Cardinal-Wood was changing her self-image more deeply than even she could perceive was akin to her soul being put in a blender. The reality was that something was mixing, transforming her blood into something different, hopefully something new. But that meant starting over, starting fresh, even if it required tearing down her foundation.

The last sketch disturbed Julia even more. An amalgam of features from the faces before was mashed together like a collage. Bianca's ponytail draped over Kyle's linebacker-sized head and ears. Zander's salesman smile was encased by Bobby's sculpted jawline. Julia could feel her own face shifting with disgust as she took notice of the sketch in full. Then she focused on the eyes Julia knew came from the sketch of her except with a twist. Dark blotches of lead were halfway covering the flaring sun pupils like they were being eclipsed. Julia couldn't find the subjective opinion that most art pieces give room for the viewer to discover. All she knew was that she was looking at an omen she didn't know the meaning of.

"Kyle, what does any of this mean?" Julia asked as she walked over to Kyle and took a knee next to him. She tried her best to formulate her words in the right order to produce an answer. "Ha-have you seen Libby since last Sunday? You said she—it—revealed secrets to you. What did *it* say?"

"You're right to be confused. Libby is much more than a human. She's closer to the divine; pronouns like he, she, and *it* aren't enough to box Libby in. I know Libby is here to help. She told me she was here to exchange all my pain for a pleasure-filled life, success, never wanting for anything. And my art would get noticed and never forgotten. I mean, look what *it* helped me do!" Kyle said, throwing both his hands forward as if he were directing Julia's eye back to the sketches on the wall or to the canvas directly in front of them. Julia didn't bother looking back. Just as Kyle had his eyes glued upward on the canvas as he knelt down, Julia kept her eyes on the fragile man her deceased cousin once called a friend.

Traces of Libby's pheromones emitted from Kyle like aftershave. As he shook his head from side to side, his illuminated eyes flickered like a bug light after it catches its prize. "That *thing* isn't offering shit but bad dreams and a funeral, Kyle. You remember what happened to Zander?"

"He couldn't handle the gift, that's all."

Julia immediately saw red. "Look, I watched my cousin's brains get guzzled like a Slurpee. Zander may have not fully known what he was getting into, but we do," Julia said, grabbing on to Kyle with two hands by the collar. Her voice steadily rose. "No matter who we saw, we watched him leave with Libby and... and..." Julia's words trailed off as her mind took over. She thought about the unique descriptions each of the employees gave and how their behaviors afterward varied just the same, how the entity not only projected itself differently to its victims but also granted what they craved the most. For what, though? "Is Libby some kind of shape-shifting alien?" she asked, her voice gradually flattening after her epiphany. She resigned herself to the fact that her own proverbial box that keeps most people's thoughts sealed in had been finally ripped into pieces.

"*Alien* would be a safe word for it. Do you believe in God?" Kyle answered Julia's question with another.

The A.R.A badge stuffed into her pocket came to mind, the one with her name, face, and designation as a field agent in dark red letters. Julia considered the Spirituality and Science wings of the building and how the search for understanding far beyond conventional reason would lead someone to connect the two, looking past numbers that compile tangible objects for the essence of creation in all things. Her belief came down to store-brand agnosticism even after growing up listening to her father's sermons. Something bigger than her was out there, watching every twinkle in the sky and listening to every beat of the heart. But genuine belief in God requires submission *to laws of nature* that humankind has recycled into inspirational phrases, cautionary stories, fairy tales, or simply forgotten. Cause and effect are a fundamental basis of our reality and the desires of the heart pull the strings connected to a person's hands.

"Whether you do or don't, the point is this: God is most certainly alien to us."

"What are you trying to say?" Julia asked, letting her hands fall back to her lap.

"There's nothing I want more than to have my art recognized, to set up pop-up shows around the city, get money from my own work, and have nothing to do with this damn fortune!" Kyle waved his arms in the air as if the whole house was to blame. "I've prayed for it! Worked for it! A commissioned piece here, an art show there. I even helped Zander with the digital art for his videos. Zander, yeah, he got it... he..." Kyle's hands pressed against the tears running down his cheeks.

"Libby didn't enhance your gift, Kyle. It's exploiting it, stealing from you the same way it stole from Zander, and it's not stopping there."

"But you don't understand. There's no time wasted discussing if the work will be worth it. The results are guaranteed, a fucking microwave success," he said, using his sleeve to wipe the remaining tears and snot from his face.

"That clock eventually hits zero, though. We've already seen it once." Julia thought of the photo of the chef's dried decomposing skin staining his angelic white suit but decided to keep that second instance to herself.

Kyle paused for a moment. "She's deep in here now," he said, hunched over with a fist in his chest, rocking back and forth like he had had the wind knocked out of him. "It's a natural high I can't escape. Fly or flop, I'd still paint and draw, but what Libby takes away she recycles back so *we* can produce more. So there's a sense of no consequence."

"What does it take, Kyle?" Julia asked as Libby's true face flashed in her memory.

"Dopamine."

"Huh?"

"That's its food. Dopamine. See, Libby isn't an alien or a god. It's a demon that answers prayers, a dope-fiend," Kyle said, nodding toward the canvas Julia had ignored.

Shades of purple layered the canvas from bottom to top. Debris from demolished buildings in the background was cloaked in the same hue. The centerpiece of the painting was a figure in a black judge's gown draped to the feet. Julia tilted her neck back to get a full perspective of the towering judge. Its face was covered in cracked flesh like the scutes of an alligator. It was the face that had been haunting Julia for the past several days. Sparkles marked galaxies encased in the demon's pupils. It had the same eyes Julia saw after her mother's face melted away in her nightmare and the ones she saw through Zander's in her avatar vision. There were the sword-like teeth forcing the mouth into a smile. And, as if the sun's rays rose above its head, a crown of seven golden spikes floated horizontally over Libby's scalp.

Julia didn't realize the knee that had been supporting her weight had buckled until her ass hit the floor. Her perspective of the room and the situation changed from the hardwood. Dancing candlelit fires shifted shadows against the sketches on the wall and a painting revealing Libby's true nature. Kyle had been not only inspired, but also enlightened. His room was a dedication to Libby, a sign of his reverence. A shrine for a demon.

# 6

# VCGFH

"So refresh me on the importance of this again," Victor Jefferson said, folding his arms across his desk at the Axiom Research Agency.

Secluded from the rest of the building's employees, drawn blinds covered giant bay windows that typically exposed Victor's office to the lab technicians of the Shadow Department, but Julia had been awarded this privacy to unveil Kyle's painting.

"It's confirmation that what I saw—experienced—was real," Julia answered, letting the blue blanket she had wrapped the painting in fall to the tiled floor, using it as the base for her display. She propped the painting up with one hand and looked down at the art while it was still under Victor's scrutiny. Julia looked into the white specs inside the black blotches used for pupils and almost got lost in the makeshift stars. A whiff of lavender grazed her nose, rising from the painting as if it were used as a scented gloss over the piece, or at least that's what Julia had hoped. Or possibly it was one of the many smells from Kyle's room that stuck to the painting. Julia shook her head at the thought of Libby's pheromone clinging to her after so much recent exposure and looked back up to Victor's unshaken, stoic shield.

"That doesn't explain why it cost five thousand dollars of the government's money."

"It's the only way Kyle would let go of it. Making money off his art is all he cares about right now." Julia thought back on the day before, after Kyle had presented his offering of praise to his new master, when the shadows had shifted across his face in rhythm with the swaying flames as he had rejected Julia's first plea to take the painting to the A.R.A. What would Bible thumpers and graph prostitutes do with this? Kyle had asked, lifting his hands up toward the masterpiece. At the time, Julia hadn't felt the need to tell Kyle why the A.R.A. needed his painting. She couldn't shake the feeling that Libby was listening, hiding behind Kyle's shining pupils. Paranoia spread throughout her body. Libby could be close or on its way. In her excitement, Julia had added a nonexistent five thousand dollars to her next bid. Kyle had eagerly pressed the painting into Julia's hands himself before receiving the money, even before Julia could call Victor to request the funds.

"Nothing wrong with an entrepreneurial spirit. I'm wondering why a picture wouldn't suffice."

"I thought this was the kind of thing that gets put in that museum."

Victor laughed. His voice weaved past tobacco-seared vocal cords as he leaned back in his chair. "No, no, no." He paused to gather himself. "The museum upstairs is for actual discoveries and the anomalies of Cardinal-Wood. Right now the only thing you have is an overpriced hobby. And once most people in the county see the last name attached, they'll figure it to be how someone copes with tragedy."

"Tragedy?" Julia asked, knowing there wasn't a county's worth of people who knew Zander and Kyle were friends.

"Yes, and one could say it's ongoing. Kyle Mitchell comes from cement royalty. His great-great-great-grandfather and seven brothers helped lay the roads of Cardinal-Wood in the 1890s. They also had a chokehold on the brick industry and had a hand in the early construction of buildings in the city. The family is one of the wealthiest in the area, probably the country as well. And they used to be one of the most abundant in numbers in the county. Joke was you couldn't go two blocks without seeing a Mitchell. Imagine how that was for them, two blocks away from being kissing cousins," Victor said, shaking his head at the thought.

Julia remembered the decor of Kyle's mansion sprinkled with photos.

Victor continued. "Well, they were thriving until the nineties. The hundred or so remaining Mitchells who hadn't yet met their ends by natural means suddenly began to be erased from this earth, if you will. House fires killing families of four. Or an eighteen-wheeler rolling over a vacationing Mitchell family of six two months later. Or fatal food poisoning from a cookout that unknowingly had a diseased cow on the menu, killing dozens. The family believed it was 'pre-seasoned,' according to reports. Or how about the Thanksgiving deep fryer explosion that left Kyle to live with his Uncle Led?"

"Oh, my god."

Victor stood up, buttoning a single gold button of his blazer. "That's my point, Ms. Thurman. Some people have more than one demon and I need you to be sure you're going after the right one." He walked over to the painting and tapped on silver painted lines staggering out of the demon's mouth. "My grandmother, rest her soul, got me a shark's tooth in a bottle back on a trip to Virginia Beach when I was seven years old. I was fascinated. Amazed. How could they fit such a sharp thing into a tiny glass container? I was so bewitched I never once considered it could be an encased carved piece of rock." Victor paused, looking at Julia now. "Ms. Thurman, I want to be bewildered again. Bring me a tooth or a piece of its crown. That would be enough for your first discovery to get its own glass jar."

"Any suggestions on how to maim a demon?"

"I believe you'll figure it out. It wouldn't hurt to go back to Mr. Mitchell's place, though. He's the only one who's given you information that's been of help. Who knows? Maybe he could help you draw this thing out.

Isn't that one of the joys of being human? Getting the opportunity to face our own proverbial demons? Using our vices, ideals, or trauma as bait for a creature hiding from the surface's light? Our hands tighten around the fishing line of the heart while being thrust left and right by a hooked Goliath. Either the line breaks from being tugged, snapped by the heart's swaying malleability or we endure the fight long enough to pull the beast out of the depths of our soul, from a place we purposely kept in darkness. Instead of feeding our demons of the deep, it becomes a conquest, a triumph, our own fuel to press forward.

Swirling between Victor's luxury cologne and Julia was a reminder that Libby was neither a lesson or far away. Lavender lifted from the painting, *or was it the blanket?* Julia knew she had more than enough bait to lure this demon out on her own.

"Have the results came back on my blood work?" Julia asked, wrapping the blue cloth over the painting once more.

"Not yet. Still analyzing how the Axiom particles are bonding to your DNA," Victor said, walking back over to his desk and pressed a button dissipating the translucent cloud within the office windows. "Any new developments I should know about? It is the main reason I brought you into this department, remember?"

Aside from the periodic goosebumps that tingled and burned between her flesh and bones, similar to what she had experienced after taking the detox pill niacin but with added heat and the info Victor was already privy to, there wasn't any new concrete evidence to share, only speculation, which she found out Victor wasn't a fan of. Julia pictured herself having a personal equivalent to a Pokémon card, similar to the ones she had briefly collected as a child. Her photo was framed in a holographic background of red, blue, or possibly purple (depending on her classification rating) accompanied with the stats of her abilities at the bottom.

*Julia Thurman. Age 26. Elevated senses (known so far): Sight, Sound, Taste, and Smell. Still Calibrating: Touch.*

Enhanced vision meant being able to detect the glow of a corrupt soul through the eyes. The infrasound of cracking glass deep within Julia's heart had shattered when an intruder had dared to hijack her soul. Her tongue could distinguish Libby's sweet gifts as lies. Her nose rivaled a bloodhound's. Four out of five sense upgrades were accounted for, whereas her shock therapy episode with Bobby felt more like a mixture of two, sight and touch. Static shock transferred between two sacks of flesh, both filled with 75 percent water, is very common, but the feeling of using Remote Desktop to gain access to someone's innermost being was new and very strange to Julia.

"Just more rocks on display—that's why I'm curious about the results," Julia said, unflinching after lying to her new boss.

Victor grinned with a smile as flat as a stale Coke. "You'll be the first to find out when they come in."

Unaccustomed to a day off on the weekend (even his time as a chaplain was a seven-day commitment), Quincy Thurman attempted to enjoy this sunny Saturday the best way he could, surrounded by stalks of green beans, unripe carrots, peppers, onions, and kale as the summer breeze carrying sounds of birds chirping hit his skin in his backyard garden.

Quincy knelt on one knee amongst the fruit of his labor, which happened to be only vegetables. A straw hat he had bought at the same farmer's market vendor where he had picked up his seeds shaded his brow from the sun but didn't prevent sweat from racing down his face. He stuck his bare hand in the soil, contemplating the pros and cons of adding strawberries or maybe a grapevine against the fence *over there*.

This was his sanctuary. The stillness comforted Quincy in a way that was hard for him to explain. There were moments when he felt peace in the absence of time, free from the bondage of twelve numbers revolving around a clock (where hours can jump forward and back depending on the place and time of year) and thriving in an environment dominated by nourishing seasonal change. Waiting for that change was another treasure to him, watching the seeds he had planted sprout, growing at a rate he'd love to one day measure in a time-lapse video. He could measure his crops and their yield in increments with the pride he imagined all other stewards of life have.

*Stewards of life?* Quincy brushed the dirt on his hands off against his lap and reached for a brown sweat rag in his back pocket that was nothing more than a cut sleeve of a T-shirt. He pressed the shredded sleeve against his damp face and turned his gaze up toward the blinding sun. Quincy's thoughts brought him to a crossroads where a person has to decide if they enjoy their hobby or if they are using it to avoid being in the present moment.

Julia, the human life Quincy was made steward over, had left for the A.R.A. earlier in the morning. She had asked him for a blanket to cover a painting involved in Zander's case, but wouldn't show it to him. "*Authorized eyes only,*" Julia had said to the guy who had gotten her the job in the first place as she reached out for the blue cover in Quincy's hand. He was sure he had the proper clearance, but why fuss? It was his day off. Just as Quincy placed the straw hat over his head before heading out into the backyard garden, without a word, Julia shuffled through the front door like a penguin holding the protected painting.

The sun's rays pushed Quincy's focus back down on the carrots in front of him and even further into his mind. He saw flashes of Julia growing up in the same manner he imagined the time-lapse video of his garden—from one to five, jumping to years eight then twelve, skipping to eighteen, and a final clip of her now at twenty-six. In each of these metaphorical snapshots of Julia, the joy in her face diminished year by year, similar to the birthday photos he'd received from Marie when he was on deployment. One year, on Julia's fourteenth birthday, Quincy received an emailed photo from Marie with the subject line "Mother–Daughter Birthday Extravaganza." Julia unenthusiastically held the handlebars of her new red mongoose bike while Marie pressed both of their faces together for the camera. The photo came with words below that sent him to his rack early that night on the ship and twisted his stomach now. *Victor was right.*

Marie's message had haunted Quincy fifteen hundred miles out in the middle of the Atlantic, just as it currently haunted him while surrounded by the growing harvest. The warning Victor had issued just before Quincy took Marie out of Cardinal-Wood with the idea that the military would work as the vehicle for their escape rang forward through time.

*"You may end up doing more damage to her if you both leave now,"* Victor had said, sitting at his desk in the old A.R.A. facility. Quincy sat across the

steel-and-wood melded desk (the pinnacle of eighties office architecture) while Marie waited outside in the car with the bags. He was flying out the next day to Chicago for boot camp and Marie had decided to drive up and live out of a motel for a month until he was finished.

"*These tests aren't going anywhere, Victor, and Marie is getting worse day by day.*" Quincy remembered saying. Both men were younger then, Victor marked by the scruff on his head that preceded complete baldness and Quincy by the absence of wrinkles on his face.

"*She'll be leaving the only place with resources that can help understand her current condition,*" Victor said.

"*This place is the cause of her condition, Victor! She never should've come back and I never should've let her stay.*" Quincy stood up and turned to leave, exhausting all his words regarding the matter.

"*The hubris that put you in front of me instead of Marie herself is also the reason you can't see that her moving here had nothing to do with you. Something in Cardinal-Wood is tugging her the way the moon pulls at the tide. Whatever is causing her to have those visions could be a sign we as a species are getting close to the next step in our evolution, a renaissance that will force people to see the spiritual and supernatural in a way that modern-day thinking has programmed the masses to ignore. And, if I'm right, Marie's condition will only worsen the longer she is away. The things she sees won't take too kindly to their human amplifier leaving town. They'll want her back.*"

"*I don't have to worry about ghosts or demons chasing us. The only one trying to raise hell in this room is you, Victor. Don't come looking for my family. I promise it won't go well for you if you do,*" Quincy finished, keeping his back toward Victor as dense silence pushed him out the door.

Marie wasn't surprised at all when Quincy told her Victor was upset to see her go. Taking the last pull of her Newport, she flicked it out of the passenger window as the car pulled out of the parking lot and lit another one. "He can go fuck himself."

Smoke rose and glazed over Marie's smooth face, circling underneath the bags of her sunken eyelids as she blew out. She had said enough for them both and Quincy couldn't think of the right words that could propel them forward into this uncharted territory they were headed toward, so he kept quiet.

Religion was always a fool's game to Quincy, who grew up going to a small Baptist church in Heathland. Located in Cardinal-Wood's countryside, the square shack painted red that sat on a hill with wooden pews on the inside while a man sat on his high horse behind a pulpit spouting his own convictions never left a desirable or believable impression on Quincy's growing mind. His position shifted after Marie began her experiments with Victor. Religion to him was still a crock of shit used to control the masses and the weak. Each region relied on its own set of tales and fables to help guide a human's moral compass, but, after seeing what Marie could do, Quincy began to consider these stories weren't myths at all but broken pieces of a puzzled truth.

For six months, in-home cameras turned their apartment into a reality TV show location set up to monitor Marie and her surroundings in various frequencies and waves. Images that captured thermal signatures revealed blotches of unconfined heat in numerous shapes around Marie throughout the day, a creature standing upright with two goat legs and the torso of a praying mantis watching Marie as she enjoyed reruns of *Jerry Springer*. A hundred legs marked in yellow rested underneath a giant oval-shaped entity wrapping around the kitchen counter like a giant centipede while Marie prepared her morning coffee.

Overnight stays were held at the A.R.A for sleep study sessions. Unlike the thermal photos Victor would review with Quincy every Friday, he could observe these firsthand. Marie's first sessions were quiet considering what they were there to do. Initially, the only strange feeling Quincy had to get over was a lab full of scientists watching his newlywed wife sleep in a blue medical gown that barely covered her ass. After multiple sessions with no findings, one night, the night that acted as a catalyst for their departure from Cardinal-Wood, all the team members began to complain of noises interfering with the study.

A tick like that of a pendulum clapping beat against the tune of Quincy's heart. The cracking sound vibrated between his eardrums and was transcribed by the recording equipment as low bungles of static. From behind the double-sided window of the observatory station, Quincy watched as Marie's eyes convulsed in REM sleep.

At first Quincy thought he heard the rumbling of the various machines plugged against the wall, until the purr grew into a brain-piercing chime that roared like a mega tuning fork from the opposite side of the window, where Marie slept. Several of the lab technicians scratched the top of their foreheads, trying to relieve the itch inside their brains from the bellowing hum. Quincy felt it too, as if something was scraping, digging between the lobes of his brain with a cerebral spade, mining for ambitions, dreams, and desires he never knew he had. Until this point, Quincy was too superficial with himself to acknowledge them.

In this rat race of a universe, where a human life could have the same value as a kibble of dog food through the lenses of chaotic evolution, Quincy's soul yearned after what every human wished they had but none could handle: the answer to all things, the functions of the world and how confusion, which is innately toxic to the human spirit, has spread through the species throughout the centuries, leading to decay. No matter what was in his way, he'd find his answers. Murder, poison, or theft, he'd do whatever it took to get what he needed. A sparkling ecstasy lit up Quincy's eyes.

*He'd even use Marie, with no regard for her life, if he had to. Victor was right to recruit her. She was like a new instrument created for discovery, a living telescope or compass of some sort, maybe more.*

Quincy inched closer to the double-sided window, pressing his nose against the glass. Thunder boomed, shaking the room Marie was in. Another rumble came, then another, and it continued like cannon fire, but Quincy knew the truth, or at least he could feel it. Something was knocking on a door he couldn't see.

Marie's eyelids peeled open. In a daze, she lifted her head off the pillow and began removing the sensor nodes stuck to her forehead that the A.R.A. was using to collect data. The banging continued, causing the lights to flicker, but none of that disturbed Marie. Her drowsy, almost dreamlike gaze was locked onto nothing. She stared off into the immediate distance, squinting her eyes as if she were trying to peek through a peephole.

The knocking raged on, thumping like a swat team ready to raid the room. Similar to a black light, Marie's gaze revealed purple ripples shooting across a transparent wall-sized door in the middle of the room. Each knock set shockwaves across the invisible door. Marie stuck one toe on the cold floor, then both feet, as she was drawn to the portal. She got so close to the nexus of two worlds that the wind from each knock shifted her hair.

A silhouette appeared in the doorway. Quincy couldn't make out what it was, but it looked large enough to show that the size of the portal was meant to accommodate what was on the other side. The silhouette eclipsed Marie's body and Quincy could see what looked like spikes lined across a scalp, like a rainbow, projected across the floor.

Marie reached forward, hovering her fingers over the lukewarm field.

"Marie, no!" Quincy called out. It would take him days afterward to admit to himself something else called out in his place.

Her fingers touched the portal, transferring an electric shock from her body. The doorway shattered like glass. A thousand pieces clattered in Quincy's ears along with the rest of the team, who fell to their knees in pain. Before the room went black and Quincy passed out, he noticed the transparent debris of the portal fade away in front of an unconscious Marie.

Quincy's cell phone rang, pulling his mind back forward forty years into the present. It was Victor.

"Hello?"

"The results are in. I thought you would appreciate the opportunity to tell her the truth as a father before I can tell her as her boss."

"Thanks." Quincy hung up the phone. Marie was right. Victor could still go fuck himself.

# 7

# JULIA OF HOUSE THURMAN

It was supposed to be a quick task, an in-and-out sort of thing. *Drop it off and go.* It was not like she was trying to sneak around either. Her father was in a trance in the back yard inspecting the quality of the soil in his hand.

She had had every intention of heading for Kyle's house after leaving the A.R.A., but a suffocating feeling wrapped itself around Julia's throat as she drove. She had a feeling it was coming from Kyle's painting that lay sideways in her backseat wrapped in the blue blanket. Julia took a detour home and found herself in her room, diving down the internet rabbit hole after one question whispered into her ear. *How long can you deny your heart?*

The question buzzed within her eardrums, drilling deep into her soul for a memory Julia purposely never revisited. The ringing in her ears drew her eyes to the backseat from the rearview mirror, locking onto the blue cover hiding the painting. She feared if she removed the cover she'd see a different painting, one that depicted her fourteenth birthday like a collage filled with trauma, confusion, and a blue bike whose color was similar to the color of the fabric staring back at her.

Deep breaths between traffic lights shattered the tone pinging in Julia's head. She was in a flow state. Seconds of directed focus connected her to the beat of her own spirit, ticking like a clock as she broke the broadcast. Once the ringing question disconnected, dropping like a bad call, the spoiled memory left an offensive taste like sour milk on her tongue. If she needed the bait, Julia had Libby saved in her favorites, readily available to summon. But the connection worked both ways. Julia's overexposure to the lavender toxin the past couple days had chipped away at her innate defense and now it was mining for an offer Julia hoped she could refuse.

After she tossed the painting into the garage, another question entered her mind, this time of her own volition. How long was Zander able to deny his heart? The answer to when could lead to where Zander first met Libby. And if Julia found the demon first, maybe she could put off confronting her own for another day.

So she scrolled and scrolled, finding nothing. Almost an hour went by as she searched through Zander's back catalog. He had uploaded over one hundred fifty videos and she was able to skip a hundred or so because Zander's eyes were already glowing on the thumbnail. Videos like "Green Cheese Sandwich" and "Egg Car Wash" took minutes of her attention because she had to wait for Zander to enter the frame after the intro to verify.

The conclusion that she was wasting time, dreaming that some cheat code clue could help claim her bounty without needing to put in the sweat necessary (either from fight or flight), was almost settled until she came across a post from Zander dated six months earlier. Julia recalled the trespassing citation Zander had nonchalantly told her he had received from this video during a conversation they had had earlier in the year. In January, she was on the fence about moving to Cardinal-Wood and, worse, back in with her father. Zander took time to sell Cardinal-Wood like a metaverse ad.

*There's so much trouble to get into here and not enough of answering for it that you won't even notice you're back living with Uncle Q. We just had a three-foot snowstorm up here and I and a few guys snuck into the water park to shoot a post for my channel.*

It was called "Winter Warzone." Zander and friends used the closed, snow-covered water park as their paintball gun battleground. Red, blue, and green paint tattered the translucent powder as the participants used slides as sniper posts and pools with caved-in tarps as the trenches.

*We only got a trespassing citation for that and I was able to go home and post the video that night! There's so much other crazy shit going on here, the cops couldn't care less about breaking into a water park.*

*Does that mean you have to care less?* she had asked, the light flavor of sarcasm on her tongue.

*I gotta accept the risks if I want to build my platform. Pushing the limit will get me in front of the most eyes, you know. When has censoring the creative spirit ever helped anyone?*

Zander's voiced lacked any similarity to the sarcasm Julia sampled to him. How deep the creative well of Zander's spirit went was in question; regardless, Julia offered him encouragement instead. *I can't wait to see you at the top.*

However, reading the comments, Julia noticed she wasn't the only one to do so.

*PlantFuel2999: Need the next vid asap!*

*SeenitTwoTimes: never thought I'd want to dive into a pool filled with snow*

*Capman: You about to put Cardinal-Wood on the map for sure bro. Funny asl*

*MybodyMyvice: The slide-by was wicked!!!*

*Live4Libby: If you need a female lead to spice up your skits email me at Live4Libby101@gmail.com. You're going to love what I have to offer*

*PetsOverPeople:* 💀 💀 💀

Julia imagined the email hooking onto Zander's heart the way it tugged on hers. How long had his eyes hovered over the hyperlink leading to the owner of the profile with the enticing offer? Did he brush it off as a joke or did he feed his curiosity with a click matching Julia's speed? What crossed his mind when the profile was missing a photo? Did he back out of the page and continue with his day? Or, like his cousin, did a low-pitch ring whistle through his ears and cause him to click on the email in the bio?

What did he type in the blank space of the body? How many words could describe the desires tucked deep into his heart? Was he able to find the words for the pleasures his heart hadn't yet yearned for, the ones tucked deep in the depths of time and experience? Or, with the flash of a blue lighted screen, was he able to glimpse a life he could never have imagined? The same rays tried piercing Julia's pupils like how a sunset tries to expose the open air or dirty laundry of a home whose window curtains are open in the dying light.

Elevated sight blocked the penetrating rays, but that could only last for so long. It felt as if specs of dirt were being peppered into her eye. Julia doubted Zander felt this pain as his fingers jumped across the keys. This resistance she felt was more closely akin to Kyle's pain.

*I'm coming for you.*

Julia sent the pride-glazed threat to Live4Libby101@gmail.com. Just as she got up to head to Kyle's house, she received an email message notification over her phone.

Mailer-daemon@gmail.com: Live4Libby101@gmail.com does not exist.

"He said he was going in to work today."

"Huh?"

"I said Kyle went into work today." Ledele stuck his head out of the entrance to his estate like an ostrich, projecting his waning vocal cords further onto the porch.

Julia heard Mr. Mitchell loud and clear. His message floated on wings of afternoon coffee. His repeating himself a few inches closer only shorted the trip. Her delay in processing Uncle Led's message came from trying to decipher what he had really said:

*Libby has mindfucked Kyle into going back to The Pit. Follow him if you dare.*

Julia tilted her head back with a sigh, grasping the estate under the sunlight. The place felt welcoming during the day, unlike the "haunted boarding school on a "hill" essence the grounds had carried the night before. Kyle's absence left a vacuum only the summer humidity could fill. Julia looked up into Kyle's window, reaching, willing for him to be up there and peek through ready to write dear old Uncle Led off as senile, waltz up to Kyle, smack the living Libby out of him, then find a way to get Victor his proof. But a human's plans are never in the Creator's final draft.

Kyle was gone and Julia had it set in her mind that she was about to walk into a trap.

"Thank you, Mr. Led. Sorry for bothering you."

Julia turned to walk to her car as Led stuck his head out of the door further, recalling Julia's attention as he spoke. "Thank you for being a friend to my nephew. He hasn't been himself since his friend passed. I-I don't recognize the boy anymore. He's sick and I'm worried I won't see him again."

"I'll bring him home."

As Julia neared The Pit she noticed a familiar car parked at the Wendy's across the street and decided it was best to take up the vantage point right next to it. She pulled into the parking spot beside Bullaby's black Challenger, only to discover his vehicle was empty.

*Maybe he went to use the bathroom.*

Julia glanced back into the fast food establishment, looking for a reward for her optimism, but she knew he wasn't in there. A void snatching the air out of the area like a black hole was coming from across the street, festering around The Pit like a cancerous tumor. Who knew how many others felt the force tugging, calling, begging, tempting them to come in? It was easy to assume Libby had pulled Bullaby into The Pit, using whatever reason he was stalking the place for and with a talon piercing his ear.

That same grip latched onto Julia's nostrils, slowly reeling her into the lavender cloud enveloping The Pit.

*Come in...*

*Come in...*

*You don't have to deny yourself any longerrrrrr...*

Libby's loop hissed inside Julia's eardrums repeatedly, bouncing off the inside of her skull like brick until she crossed The Pit's threshold. Sudden silence greeted her in the waiting area. The space was empty. No host took up their position on the front line. Only her footsteps echoed through the empty corridor as they pressed against the red carpet.

Between paces Julia heard a faint clatter of forks coming from beyond the curtain. Light from the dining area sliced the divide of the curtain. Julia stood there for seconds that felt like minutes, hesitant to go through. The lavender toxin in the air was thick, shortening Julia's breath as if she was breathing smog from a fire. It reminded her of a video she had seen of a Good Samaritan running inside a burning home to save a toddler neighbors said was left inside the house. The man rushed outside the flaming home, holding the kid like a football. Both came out of the house with minor burns and soot covering their bodies. It was reported the Samaritan died days after the deed from respiratory complications but the boy was fine. Julia disregarded the pessimistic lesson of that news story as she leaned forward, squinting through the opening in the fabric.

Julia expected more customers to be seated in the dining area on a Saturday evening. The scraping of silverware over each plate was louder than the whispers of the patrons' conversations. It was like everyone was sharing a special secret after each bite. While verifying Kyle's absence, she lost count at twenty-one customers and six employees in the space once sweat from her forehead fell into her eye.

The lavender toxin's prying persisted. It had started off as another voice, but one Julia was familiar with, reverberating back from her past like a scream on top of a mountain. It was Marie trying to reach her.

*Juliaaa...*

*Juliaaa...*

*Juli—*

Deep breaths that reached the pit of the soul shattered the broadcast once again with focused precision. Libby was close and the longer Julia waited, the more strongly she felt the tug of the spider creeping on its web. Her only option now was to fish Kyle out of the back kitchen and employee area, but that meant going deeper into The Pit.

Julia parted the curtain with her hand as she crossed into the dining area. A no-named waiter stood around a table of four scrolling through their phone, unconcerned by the customers' piling empty plates. Another employee was seated at the bar amongst a mix of suits and construction workers, holding a drink high in the air. Julia was familiar with her, though. Even as the worker's back was facing Julia, the braids and the moonstone ring on the hand holding a double shot made it obvious. Tiffany (the crystal girl with green braces) readied her lungs to make a toast.

"We've all been given a gift." Tiffany spun around from the bar to face the room. She chugged the double shot of a clear liquid—either vodka or tequila— before finishing her toast and slammed the glass down on the counter in silent protest for another drink. A female customer, a member of the suit crew, loaded Tiffany up with another drink while she continued her speech. Julia slowly crept around the dining hall of madness without drawing attention to herself. All she needed to do was make it to the kitchen.

Tiffany continued with a new double shot in hand. "This gift comes with purpose or pleasure. What's life? It's but an option. Create or consume. Inspire or extinguish. Victim or villain. Always wanting something for nothing. Honestly, humanity's moral compass has been fucked since the beginning. I'm surprised you all even made it this far." Her voice started to develop a manic pitch and a whistle-like tone sounded off along with her words. Each step became a slog in quicksand as Julia weaved around the crowd. The kitchen door was just over *there!*

"Historical texts from thousands of years ago that acknowledged the spirits and supernatural conditions of life have all been watered down to vibes and laws of attracting the life you want, the car you want to drive, or who you want to fuck. Did those people know less than a generation who can't even build their own fire? Even today, I've been eroded to just a myth. I'm nothing more than a word that lost it's power and yet you all feed me every day. Your leaders told you that you use only 10 percent of your brain to keep you from striving to use more, then gave you toys so you'd use even less. My gift is not a distraction but one's ultimate wish. No more doom scrolling to pass the time. No more looking and saying, *oh if I had what they had I'd—*." Tiffany swayed her head side to side to the tune of her own beat. "Or you could even see your dear old dead drunk of a mother again."

All those with listening ears robotically turned to face Tiffany in one unified shift. Julia, now standing at the entrance to the kitchen behind the bar, couldn't move any further. Tiffany stared down at her from a barstool, foaming at the mouth in a frenzied rage like a dictator who has just finished a polarizing speech before executing a traitor.

Julia thought of moments of mercy she had many times before fully killing a bug she swatted from her arm as it fluttered on the ground in panic. What was it thinking as it saw its end coming in the form of a giant white napkin? What was the fly caught in the spider's web thinking as it buzzed in frantic fear when it saw an eight-legged beast descending from the shadows? These questions floated around now because fear froze her too.

Everyone's eyes in the room began to glow in Libby's signature light, shining on Julia like an ant under a microscope. She was on display like a kid nervous from the bright lights of the talent show stage, while a flash mob of Libby drones glared at her with their high beams on. They all spoke in a unified voice that cut through the air and pierced Julia's eardrums.

"Well, lucky for you, Julia! I exist in the equation of all things." The mob spoke with the energy of a church choir. Julia could feel her mind splitting from the unified song. Stuck in the moment, she felt as if chunks of her brain that held a long-suppressed memory were being extracted, carved, and catered for Julia to get lost in forever.

Julia reached for the side of her head to stop the blender in her brain. How had she gotten caught in a trap like this, surrounded by a Libby militia? She had seen the light in the drone's eyes but, as her hand slipped across the sweat on her forehead, the revelation became clear. She felt like a crab being boiled slowly, killed without her awareness for the optimal flavor. The voice box Libby used for it's speech confirmed, at least partially, Julia's brilliant decision not to call Kyle before searching for him. That returned email was no mistake but a display of Libby's control over the so-called toys of technology. If it was a dope fiend or the embodiment of lust, more than the word, then it would see screens of various sizes as doors to the foundation of the soul, specifically, the brain guiding it. From the toxins surrounding every drone Julia had come into contact with, every TV, computer, or phone screen her eyes watched between; planted seeds inside that Libby could harvest whenever it pleased.

"Why here? Why now?" Julia forced her questions out while keeping her knees from buckling. Marie's voice whispered through the banging in Julia's head. Julia could feel her consciousness slipping away, back into a day in the past she intentionally never revisited. Back to a conversation she wished she never had after a question she wished she never asked. Focusing on Marie's whisper and the approaching hell of a memory weakened Julia's knees more. She couldn't fall down now. Libby's toxin had finally broken through all of Julia's natural defenses and she couldn't bear to imagine what would happen to her if she hit the floor surrounded by the drones. It would be mutilation or worse. She had to stay standing.

"You're the one who wishes for a world where loved ones tell you the actual truth and not one that fits their flaws, for leaders who don't use deception to hide the sum of their game. I know the words from your heart that have never reached your lips. And you know I can give it. It's our parents who love us and lie to us first, Julia. You're not the only one who wants things to be different. I think all of creation could sympathize with that." The room rumbled as Tiffany led the Libby drone choir on its tirade.

"No, why Cardinal-Wood? Why are you here now?" Julia's vision blurred. One eye drifted to the past, watching her mother's face lying next to Julia the morning of her fourteenth birthday. The other eye stayed locked on Tiffany and the drones behind her. Julia was almost gone. Her consciousness was splitting from the waking world and she could do nothing about it.

"The answers are one and the same. It's like asking why the wind is blowing or if the sun will be in the sky during the day. The only difference between here and New York, LA, and the world is that Cardinal-Wood's air is filtered from a place of existence humans have long forgotten. And now I have *another* pioneer meddling in my affairs. The world has gotten this close to destruction because I've fulfilled the desires of the powerful and weak. The self-serving cancer ingrained in the human genome has been allowed to thrive because I fed it. Kings and castles have burned over a woman. Nations have fallen to the lustful eye of the conqueror. And now a billion souls wish for everything but a way out of the box their screens have put them in!" The room roared, causing pictures to fall off the wall and glasses around the room to shatter.

Suddenly the saloon-style door of the kitchen behind Julia swung open with enough force to send her crashing to the floor. Too weak to pick herself up and wincing from the pain, numbness, and confusion her body was going through, Julia had a chance to experience one last emotion before her end: torment.

Detective Bullaby, the high beams of his eyes bright, led the procession out of the kitchen He was followed by Bobby, Bianca, and, finally, Kyle. Julia used her elbows to drag herself backward on the floor as Libby's honorary guard entered the room. Bullaby stood in a black suit drenched in sweat. Bobby by his side still enchanted with ethereal beauty. Bianca looked almost as malnourished as Zander had on the coroner's table. It was as if she was imprisoned in The Pit, forced to do her managerial duties and nothing else. And then there was Kyle, whose head nodded zombie-like on top of his large slouching shoulders.

Julia was reminded once again of how late she was to save someone. How incapable she was of protecting anyone, even herself. She had let grudges and transgressions of the past mold her future. What was living if she couldn't save the ones she loved like her mother and Zander, if she couldn't give them the world, heal them of their pain, or take their suffering away? And it wasn't even just loved ones, but also the deserving, the sick, the needy—Bobby, Bullaby, Bianca, and Kyle. Maybe Libby was right and what it could give had to outweigh how she'd been living. She had never believed in this world anyway. Finally, she closed her eyes, refusing to participate any longer, and drifted away into darkness with thundering laughter in the background.

"Good morning, baby girl. It's your special day."

Julia's eyes opened to Marie lying in her bed, watching her as she woke up. Before her eyes adjusted to the light, Julia knew where she was from the scent of tequila on her mother's breath. More specifically, she knew when. It was twelve years ago, the morning of Julia's fourteenth birthday, and, just as they had back then, Marie's strawberry margarita-coated words pried her eyelids opened.

"Happy birthday, Julia," Marie said, placing a hand on Julia's cheek.

"You couldn't wait until after you took me to the store?" Julia said, swatting Marie's hand from her face as she sat up. Marie slid her back up against the baseboard, calm and smooth.

"Don't worry, baby, we can still make it. I have your favorite pancakes ready downstairs."

The option of pancakes almost intrigued Julia until another wave of strawberry (was it from a cocktail mix or the real fruit?) hit her nose. "Even though you don't mind feeding your future liver cancer, I'd rather not die and be a statistic on my birthday. I can take the bus."

"How about I let you drive? It's only ten minutes to the mall. We can get your bike and get out."

Again Julia was tempted, but her teenage tongue couldn't hold back its fire. "You should've thought of that before you guzzled down your happy hour drink before eight a.m. I can't get one day with you normal, sober, not broken?"

Marie slapped Julia on the same cheek, shuffling Julia's already messy morning hair. She slapped her again and watched Julia hold her face in shock as she attempted to hold back tears. Her mouth widened as if she was trying to process how or why her mother struck her so fast.

"You're right. I'm broken. I'm never sober and never will be normal, but that doesn't mean I don't love you. And that doesn't mean you can talk to me any way you want. I am your mother and you have my blood. If you think I'm broke, then think of how you would fix me and see if that works for you."

"That's a lot of words for trying to say you're simply drunk," Julia said, fire still on her tongue and tears still rolling down her eyes.

Marie shook her head with a smirk and pushed herself up off the bed. Julia shifted back as if she was bracing herself for another slap that Marie had no energy for. "When you can provide for yourself, then you can learn the truth about me. There's so much you and your little mind don't know about the world that if I told you, you would still need my shelter and protection. I'm the first person who's going to love you and lie to you, and you have to accept it as one and the same. You can hate me for it all you want now, but eventually you'll understand." Marie walked to the door. "We're leaving in an hour. I'll be sober then." She finished and shut the door behind her. Julia's vision went black again.

She was stuck in this moment for what felt like an eternity: opening her eyes to her mother's margarita breath, a slap on the face (more like two), the morning of her birthday, and a lecture about love, lies, and blood that ended with a slammed door whose noise acted like a director's clapboard signaling *Action!* for the next looping scene.

Julia's mind started realizing the prison trapping her spirit around the tenth replay. Slowly she was remembering how the rest of that day had played out, with her mom buying her the blue mongoose bike she was eyeing at the mall months before. Julia remembered taking a photo with the bike for her dad, then leaving as Marie typed the email to enjoy her gift far away from her mother. She had returned later that evening to find Marie passed out on the couch.

What charges had condemned her to this jail? She remembered her judge that promised freedom but only delivered atonement with a gavel. *Libby.* As years went on in the nightmare, Julia wondered how much time had gone by in the waking world. Minutes, hours, days? Was she dead? Or was Libby using her body like a puppet the same way she had Zander's?

*Zander*. She had almost forgotten how she got here. She was upset at herself for not being there for him when he needed it most, the same way she hated Marie for her own neglect. What constructive words would she use to coax her mother up now since she'd completed her rite of passage into womanhood after finally paying her own water bill for a few semesters? These words should help Julia herself if genetics worked the way Marie mentioned. How about a little discipline to put the bottle down? Or should it be the discipline to listen to that slight tapping of the soul, knocking like a pendulum? The kind of tick that centers the mind in the body. A sound that can be easily drowned out from lack of focus or desired awareness. Or with understanding and a hug would she tell her mother she was right? And thank her for keeping the monsters of this world hidden away, no matter why she decided not to confront them? Julia's heart said yes and the fabricated walls of her prison crumbled.

More darkness. Julia opened her eyes to a familiar void with mirrored glass at her feet. Thousands of mirrors, possibly more, hung in place, unlike Bobby's lone frame from last time. It was like she was between realms, a place where Libby managed its network. She was free in this space, able to move up and down the aisles of gold-framed mirrors like the wind, or like a virus. A sharp pain shot through her side as if she had been kicked in the ribs. She pressed her hand against the throbbing pain and moved on.

She watched various people, young and old, bang away on their glass cell. What was on the other side of their panels? What agonizing hell had they signed up for under the guise of entitlement? She wanted to break them all out, to yell to them there was a way out of the maze, but she had a feeling she was short on time and her message would be as soundless as their screams.

Julia glimpsed familiar faces near the spot she began exploring. The Pit's staff, Bianca, Bobby, Tiffany, Kyle, and Detective Bullaby were all in one row. She wasn't leaving without them. With words useless in this vacuum, Julia walked over to

Detective Bullaby's mirror with the intention to shatter it. What was the worse that could happen? She needed to shatter her own to get out, right?

She touched the glass and like a thin layer of ice left over a car window after rolling down, it collapsed. Bullaby didn't appear next to Julia but she didn't stop. She moved on to Kyle. She felt a spark after touching Bullaby's cage that reminded her of the first time you shock your crush with static shock. It just felt right. So she touched Kyle's mirror and moved on once it fell.

Then she went to Tiffany, who she should've started with. If she cut off the demon's head, its entire network should crash. She tapped Tiffany's mirror as she pounded away, but the mirror shattered like normal.

Two more sharp pains came in her side. This time the pains were on both the left and the right, slouching Julia over as she gasped for air. It felt like she was being trampled on, but she continued to Bianca. Before she could put a finger up, Libby shoved Bianca out of the way and hissed a sound that shook the space it commanded. The vibrating shook the space like an earthquake, sifting Julia out like a filter. Her consciousness fell back into her body inside The Pit.

"Ahhhhh!" The room roared a painful ballad followed by the sound of crashing tables and chairs.

Julia regained consciousness inside The Pit. A chorus of moans was coming from around her like a pack of wolves in pain. She stood up and saw Kyle, Detective Bullaby, and Tiffany slowly gathering themselves off of the floor in a daze. They were surrounding Julia as if they were to blame for what felt like broken ribs. It was as if Libby had made them take turns kicking Julia to literally boot her out of its system. The rest of the customers in the room began to compose themselves as if they had just finished one unified vomit. Bianca reached for Julia's leg from the ground, too frail to pick herself up.

"You bitch!" Libby yelled from its proxy's mouth.

Julia kicked Bianca on the nose, between her high-beam eyes, until she let go. By then Bullaby was on his feet. Julia squeezed his hand. "Grab Kyle. I got Tiffany. We have to run now!"

# 8

# WATER WOOD ROYALE

They ran across the street toward Julia's car. Julia tugged Tiffany along using her own momentum to keep the girl's wobbly knees under her. She turned back to see Bullaby with enough strength now to carry Kyle with one arm around his shoulder. She also saw Bianca, Bobby, and the swarm of drones rush to the entrance and stop.

Julia unlocked the car door, shoving Tiffany into the backseat. Bullaby tossed Kyle into the car with the same vigor and hopped into the passenger seat as Julia started the car. She sped off into the sunset, watching Libby's drones wail in anger, piling up at the door, reaching and foaming at the mouth, but they didn't leave the building. As Julia watched their glowing eyes disappear in the rearview mirror, she figured the drones didn't chase them because they were instructed not to.

Julia was seated in the kitchen of her father's house along with the other three. Surrounded by silence, they bonded by the drained, confused, yet kindred spirit all recently freed captives share until Quincy poured a glass of water for Julia out of the fridge.

"Here you go, baby girl."

122

Julia extended her arm for the cup but quickly pulled back from the pain in her side. "Shit!" The moments of relaxation wore off the adrenaline masking her pain.

Quincy sat the glass on the table and got down on one knee. "I gotta take you to the hospital ASAP."

"No! Libby is still out there," Julia said, sliding the chair back and standing in one motion. She held a face of resilience as pain jolted through her body. "It's still out there and I don't know what's about to happen to all of those under its control at The Pit. And why didn't they follow us?"

"How do we know they didn't?" Bullaby's skepticism caused all eyes to shift in the room.

"Because Libby was about to feed. It's got all the ingredients together for a major buffet. All it was looking for was Julia as it's main course," Kyle explained with his head slouched over.

"Can I get water, sir?" Bullaby asked, slightly raising the hand that wasn't rubbing his forehead.

"Sure," Quincy answered, focusing on Julia for a few more moments before walking away. He decided to get the others some water too.

"How do you know Libby is ready to eat Kyle?" Julia walked over to him. It was her turn to kneel but she did it slow.

"Because it said if I got you to show up, then I wouldn't have to go."

"Go where?"

"Water Woods Park."

"What the fuck was about to eat me? What are you people talking about?" Tiffany asked, hysterically rubbing her moonstone ring.

Quincy brought the rest of the group their water.

"Yeah, enough of this shit. Pardon my language, sir, but what is going on? One second I'm staking out The Pit and the next I'm running out with you surrounded by lunatics," Bullaby stated. Now both of his hands were on his head trying to grasp the situation.

"Don't you know a little of what's going on? Weren't you still investigating my cousin's death?" Julia asked, a little confused.

"What? No! Nothing has changed about that. I was investigating your tax-evading boss! After interviewing all the employees, I caught a glimpse of her roster and the numbers weren't adding up. She's claiming more people than she's paying. Now tell me what's going on."

Julia told Bullaby and Tiffany all of what she knew about the demon named Libby and its food of choice dopamine. She decided to reveal her involvement with the A.R.A. on a need-to-know basis.

"So, this monster—"

"Demon," Julia and Kyle said simultaneously, not shying away from the creature's true nature.

"Okay. It wants our dopamine?"

"Is it that hard to believe? You were so Captain America you wanted to bring Bianca down and Libby started using your brain for soup," Julia rebutted.

"That doesn't make sense. I just want to live. There's nothing wrong with that. I'm just working there to pay for community college."

"What if you found something that could give you that faster than one of your rocks? All it takes is a whisper for it to get into your head, or for someone who's in its control to sway you. I saw Bobby doing it firsthand," Julia said, crossing her arms and pacing the kitchen.

"That's why it wants you, Julia. It needs to stop you. You're like some sort of disrupter to it. I even felt it yesterday when you came by. Libby did too."

"Felt what?"

"Like a static fuzz in my head. Almost like my brain was tuning itself to think on its own again. I dunno."

Julia did, though. She turned back toward her father.

"You knew about Mom's abilities, didn't you?"

Quincy froze. His heart was more solid than the ice melting in Julia's untouched glass.

"Baby girl, we didn't know what to do back then. Your mother was scared."

"So ya'll ran away?"

"We left for a normal life. We left to start a family."

"You started a career and left Mom to rot."

"How dare you say that! I did what I thought was best! She didn't fight me on it either! You have no idea what you're talking about."

"If either of you had some fight built in instead of flight, or a little courage, then she would've been able to confront her gift instead of being crippled by it." Julia paused for a moment. "I know what I have to do."

"You're not leaving." Quincy moved in front of the hallway to the front door.

"It's not your choice. If we both have a lesson to take from here, then it never was yours to make in the first place."

Quincy froze again. The fire in Julia's spirit thawed away his remaining shame. "I-I can't let you go alone then."

"She won't be. I'll go with her," Kyle said, lifting his head.

"I need to go alone," Julia said, standing in the center of the huddle. "Who knows if Libby can't regain control over any of you after I disconnect you? It's not like you all lost your separate desires. And it knows that."

"A little self-control goes a long way," Bullaby said, standing up from the table. Everyone's head turned. "Oh please, I'm fucking going," he said, swiftly moving his blazer at the waist to flash his gun.

"I'm not staying behind. It's not an option. We have to stop this thing for Zander," Kyle said, staring at Julia in a way that told her they were bonded by the same goal.

"Okay, then. Dad, call Victor and get Tiffany to the A.R.A. He'll know what to do next."

"Wait. You people are nuts. What does a research agency full of scientist and pastors have to do with all of this?" Bullaby said with his trademark cynicism.

Julia ignored the substance of his statement. "I'll fill you in on the way. We're going to the water park."

Welcome to Water Woods Park!

The sign's rainbow-colored letters hung like a banner over a picture depicting flooded woodlands and water slides descending from various trees as if ripped straight from a fairytale. Julia cut the headlights off, double-parking her car at the top of the hill that overlooked the waterpark and its facilities.

"You gotta be kidding me. This all has to be a joke. You know I'm an *X Files* fan, right?" Bullaby said. "And you work for these people?"

Julia fumed. "What's the joke? That your government actually believes in the supernatural and puts tax dollars into researching it? Or that you didn't think it did? My badge is in the glove box if you want to see."

Bullaby didn't bother. "What's next?"

"Kyle, Zander recorded a video here but he had to break in to do it. Do you know how he broke in?" Julia asked, turning toward the backseat.

"Yeah. The construction site down there. He made a hole in the fence." Kyle leaned forward and pointed. "It's a new slide they're building, The Atlantis Lookout."

His hand guided their eyes into the darkness. Moonlight reflected off of the large sectioned pools and metallic slides below. The tallest attraction in the park, boxed in by a fence and a drained pool, was a lookout tower with pieces of the unfinished slide stacked next to yellow construction trucks illuminated by the pale satellite.

"You know why Libby is bringing them here? It didn't need to draw Zander away."

"I can't say. But you're right. It doesn't feel like it would need to round up its food. Libby is like a plague once in your head. It was eating us already."

*Go.*

Julia thought of Victor's explanation of the thin veil between the natural and supernatural elements of this Earth. Then she considered how Cardinal-Wood's Axiom particles could make that veil even thinner. *Go!* gained a new meaning.

"C'mon."

The trio left the car and began their walk into the thick night, toward the park.

"I think Libby is trying to take her drones somewhere. And I mean somewhere that's not Earth," Julia whispered.

"Hell?" Bullaby asked equally low.

"Wherever Libby calls home. Whatever is going on in Cardinal-Wood, it must be the right conditions for it to—."

"Try something new," Kyle chimed in.

When they got to the bottom of the hill, their feet locked in place all at once. Ten to fifteen cars were sprinkled around a parking lot of what should've been an empty park. Julia nudged Kyle, snapping him out of a dazed fear and reminding him with a nod to lead them toward Zander's hole in the fence. He pushed forward slowly.

Julia used the light from her phone pressed at the ground to guide their feet. They rounded the far corner of the parking lot into the construction area. At the fence Julia could immediately smell a lavender fog permeating through the metal openings. She could trust herself. After escaping Libby's hold on her own, she felt a new security and a new form of control over her abilities. But she didn't trust how far that extended. How long would Kyle or Bullaby be able to keep control of their own heads?

Kyle searched for the opening. "You guys ready? All I need to do is get close enough to touch Libby and I think I can sever its connection to Earth, or at least dull whatever signal boost it's getting in Cardinal-Wood."

Bullaby nodded. "I got your six."

"Over here." Kyle lifted the cut opening in the fence as his confirmation.

Dozens of footprints led them through the construction site as if Libby had guided her drones through the same opening Zander used months before. Julia cut off her phone's light, now able to trust only the cover of the night as they moved forward.

In the pool area, Julia ducked behind a life jacket station just as she noticed a group of silhouettes gathered twenty feet ahead at the lifeguard tower. Kyle and Bullaby quickly followed suit.

A celestial light caused by the reflection of the moon bouncing off the blue water acted as a spotlight for a shadowy figure standing on the tower. The being took a position on the railing like the pope atop the Vatican. Julia saw galaxy-like pupils blazing from the tower, piercing the night. While the swaying of the water constantly shifted the direction of the moon's rays, the face surrounding those eyes shifted too, morphing with the wind into beautiful faces with smiles to die for, and handsome ones whose grins were formed to deceive. Young and old, all but one of the faces were familiar to Julia, the face Libby appeared to her with, the woman with the black locks.

The wind shifted again, covering Libby in the shadows once more. A whistle blew soft in the sky and the night swayed, stilling the light back onto Libby who disregarded its masks for its true nature. Dry cracked skin resembling grey scales covered its face. Black lips, darker than oil, tried to contain teeth as sharp as swords that spread its jaw into a wide, sickening smile. A crown of seven gold floating rainbow spikes over its head glimmered like the North Star. Talons on Libby's hands scrapped the railing of the tower, echoing a screech to the watching crowd.

"Look at that," Bullaby whispered.

"You can see Libby?" Julia turned, startled.

"Yeah, I mean, it's beautiful." His eyes began to shimmer. She was running out of time.

"Kyle. Kyle!" Julia snapped but kept her voice low. Kyle's eyes began to sparkle too. She had overestimated her abilities. Any nullification frequency she was emitting must have been null and void the closer she was to Libby and not a proxy.

"Your audience is welcomed, Julia. Kyle did well to bring you here." Kyle's mouth began the song of Libby's choir. Its essence standing on the lifeguard post remained still while a hundred pairs of glowing pupils turned to face Julia like a pack of rabid raccoons. Kyle and Bullaby reached for separate arms and began to drag Julia through Libby's attendants.

"How? He wasn't under your control. I'm sure of it," she said as they threw her at the base of Libby's pseudo throne. She looked to her left and saw Bianca and Bobby in the same stupor.

*"We have to stop this thing for Zander."* Kyle repeated in a mocking fashion what he had said an hour earlier, but she knew it wasn't him speaking.

The beast moved its obsidian lips. "I told you I know the words of your heart that haven't reached your lips yet. You humans are so fragile, easily falling for your wants instead of doing what you need. Even without my presence, Kyle remembered my whisper like a memory of a wind chime. No one you save from me is truly safe. Let me show you." Libby's voice chimed loud like a mega tuning fork, vibrating the water.

Libby floated down, robed in darkness. "I need to feed before opening the Corridor." Libby said, reaching for Bianca's head and clutching both cheeks with its talons.

"Wait!" Julia screamed, stretching out a hand only to receive dread in return.

Libby's jaw opened as wide as a whale's before it sank its sword teeth into Bianca's skull, penetrating deeper than bone. For a few seconds a sound similar to a car's tires grinding in mud roared. Bianca's body decomposed right in front of Julia. Libby tossed her aside like a Capri Sun and let out a sigh of refreshment.

"I want you to watch." Libby drifted in Julia's direction and grasping her face in its cold, sharp claws. Libby's galaxy pupils looked up into the sky where they belonged and summoned a purple teardrop. It fell like a shooting star from the sky or like that one lonely raindrop that precedes a storm. As it reached the ground, the trail behind it cut a seam through the air that ripped time and space.

The veil began to unfold. Julia's eyes widened as the air was pulled from her chest. She could not scream loudly enough to match the terror she felt as the natural world slid aside like a dual sliding door entrance to a grocery store. The Corridor's entrance reached high, high enough that it hurt Julia's neck to see it all as Libby tilted her head. Its opening was as wide as two eighteen-wheelers, cutting off half of the pool and the area behind the lifeguard tower.

Inside Julia saw a purple-hued dystopia. Demolished buildings were glossed over by a color only the most beautiful sunset could produce but the sky was pitch black. It almost looked like there was no sky at all. A loud gust of wind blew from inside like a tornado rumbling through a canyon or a multitude of screams.

Libby waved its free hand and all the drones, minus Kyle, Bobby, and Bullaby, began their passage to the other side.

"Please! You don't have to do this!" Julia pleaded to the demon. Tears formed in Julia's eyes. She couldn't see what happened to those who went to the other side. The Corridor just rippled like water as they went through.

"Oh, but I do. I can't pass up this opportunity to order takeout. No human has crossed over. Who knows how long my food will last over there? My stay in Cardinal-Wood was cut short once you arrived. If it had not been for you, this whole county would be going home with me!"

Bobby, Kyle, and Bullaby each took a step toward the Corridor.

Closer.

And closer.

Ever so close now, their faces were touching the veil.

It sucks that sometimes life comes down to this one simple truth. If you believe in the gifts planted in yourself with the same intensity that the enemy uses to try to stop you, then you can achieve anything.

Julia believed. It was in her blood bubbling up in the form of a whisper out of her spirit. It was a feeling that afterward she could explain only as that inclination to make the first move or taking a leap of faith to move to a strange county. The tiny hairs on her arms stuck up as her elevated spiritual senses converted the touch of her hand and the 55 percent water comprising her body into a super conductor. She pressed a finger into Libby's robe. A delayed surge propped a prideful smirk onto the beast's face before Julia defeated the demon with a touch.

Libby began to shatter and implode simultaneously. It let go of Julia as pieces of its black cloak fell, but they were being consumed by its void like a vacuum before hitting the ground. A golden spike from Libby's crown broke away, falling at Julia's feet. She held it tight, even as it sliced through her palm.

"Julia!" Kyle ran over and helped Julia to her feet. He was followed by Bullaby and Bobby, who was already gaining his weight back. She had severed their connection.

The relief was short lived. Libby latched its talon onto Kyle's forearm, spraying blood onto Julia's face. Libby held onto Kyle, its black robe fluttering like a giant moth or a gothic kite struggling to maintain altitude as Kyle was its remaining anchor in the physical world.

Julia tossed the golden spike far behind her toward the life vest booth, hoping there'd be enough distance between it and the implosion. She reached for Kyle with both hands and held tight.

"Ahh, shit! Oh, god, Julia please don't let me go! I'm not trying to die like this!" Kyle screamed, his eyes bloodshot red in pain. Julia could tell he was being split in two.

"You gotta let go! You're hurting him too!" Bullaby cried, trying to pull Julia away.

She watched as the Corridor began to close, dragging the remaining pieces of Libby and Kyle back toward it.

"Please, Julia." She heard Kyle's whimper through the thundering wind.

"I'm sorry, Kyle. I promise I'll find a way to—."

The Corridor sucked the remaining pieces of Libby inside, tugging Kyle right out of Julia's hands before she could finish. The gateway to the unknown world closed and the wind stood still.

# 9

# HEAVY IS THE HEAD

6 months later.

Merry Christmas!

*And this Christmaaass will beee*
*A very special Christmaahaaaas for meeeeee yea!*

Julia smiled from behind the bar, taking in the people gathered at The Pit's Christmas celebration. It was a heavy smile, but a smile Donny Hathaway's song had lifted on millions of faces like clockwork each year. She couldn't attribute all of her happiness to Donny's smash hit, though. She took a deeper look around.

She watched Bobby sharing a drink with Tiffany and the rest of the staff. A bright smile displayed he was comfortable in his glow.

"Can I get a double of tequila?" a voice called over the music. It was Bullaby in a Christmas sweater.

"I'll have to get the bartender for that." Julia smiled as she reached for his hand. "How've you been?"

"Good. Good." He looked around to see if anyone was paying attention. "You get any news on if I got that interview?"

She shook her head softly. "There's no openings right now. It's gotta mean something that you're the first person I call now, right? What's wrong with keeping open communication between CWPD and the A.R.A?" Julia asked sarcastically, patting Bullaby on the shoulder.

"Yeah, yeah. I want in on the action too, that's all."

"Trust me. There's more than enough."

Donny Hathaway's music continued. "So I like what you've done with your caregiving allowance," Bullaby said, waving a hand around The Pit.

"Mr. Led signs off on everything. Plus he gave me a large sum up front. This came from my portion."

"How much the old man give you? He's like C-W royalty."

"I could've bought the CWPD and then The Pit."

"Say no more."

"Thank you, though. For helping with the process I mean. Because Mr. Led has no relatives, his fortune would've gone to the state. Now I can have it waiting for Kyle when I find him."

"Julia." Bullaby softened his eyes.

"It was nice seeing you, Detective, but I have to go."

"It was nice seeing you too."

Julia grabbed her coat and gave Tiffany a nod as she went to the front door. She had assigned her closing duties after the party as well as made her co-owner.

Dodging dozens of ugly Christmas sweaters, Julia made it to the front door, where Victor and her father were holding a conversation.

"Where you off to in such a hurry?" Quincy asked. "It's not even ten o'clock yet."

"I want to go play a game of chess with Mr. Led before it gets too late," Julia said. "Then I have to go into the office."

Victor looked into the distance, unbothered.

"No way, Julia. It's a holiday. You gotta celebrate the small things, baby girl."

"I understand, but not right now. Merry Christmas." She gave him a hug and a kiss on the cheek. "You as well, Victor," she said, giving him a half bow.

"A word with you outside, please?" Victor asked.

"Sure," Julia said, walking out into the snow.

It was cold enough to snow but not cold enough to freeze outside during a quick talk. Or so Julia hoped.

"I left a file on your desk. A farmer down in Heathland may know something about your Corridor."

"Thank you, Victor."

"No, thank you. And welcome to the team. I left you a present in the museum."

Julia strolled into the A.R.A. building shortly after midnight following her game of chess with Mr. Led. She went through the museum that had held her in awe months ago, thinking it had almost lost its magic until she saw a bright red bow on display next to an oversized grape. It was a golden spike propped up like it was a delicate feather. Its label read: *Gold alloy with cosmic substances unknown to Earth*. Julia's heart read something different. *In the Spirit, I can do all things*. And then she went to work.

THE END